It would be utter madness. He was about to disappear off to another country. He could promise her nothing even if he'd wanted to.

But it would also be fantastic. Dynamite. It would certainly beat chopping logs the whole weekend. It *had* been too long since he'd had a woman in his bed, and who knew when the opportunity would next arise? Who knew when he'd have the time?

Desire began to pound through him and his control began to unravel.

"Matt?" she said with a sexy kind of breathiness that had him envisaging her saying his name in a whole lot of other ways.

With the images that spun through his head, the last vestiges of his resistance crumbled and Matt gave in. He wanted her. She wanted him. Why shouldn't they go for it, and to hell with the consequences?

Ruthlessly ignoring the little voice inside his head demanding to know what on earth he thought he was doing, Matt tilted his head and gave her a slow smile. "I think you should stay."

LUCY KING spent her formative years lost in the world of Harlequin romance novels when she really ought to have been paying attention to her teachers. Up against sparkling heroines, gorgeous heroes and the magic of falling in love, trigonometry and absolute ablatives didn't stand a chance.

But as she couldn't live in a dream world forever, she eventually acquired a degree in languages and an eclectic collection of jobs. A stroll to the River Thames one Saturday morning led her to her very own hero. The minute she laid eyes on the hunky rower getting out of a boat, clad only in Lycra and carrying a three-meter oar as if it were a toothpick, she knew she'd met the man she was going to marry. Luckily the rower thought the same.

She will always be grateful to whatever it was that made her stop dithering and actually sit down to type Chapter One, because dreaming up her own sparkling heroines and gorgeous heroes is pretty much her idea of the perfect job.

Visit her at www.lucyking.net.

THE CROWN AFFAIR

LUCY KING

~ Young, Hot & Royal ~

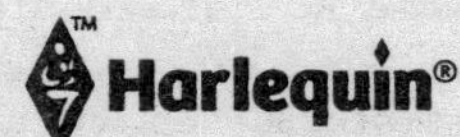

TORONTO NEW YORK LONDON
AMSTERDAM PARIS SYDNEY HAMBURG
STOCKHOLM ATHENS TOKYO MILAN MADRID
PRAGUE WARSAW BUDAPEST AUCKLAND

Recycling programs
for this product may
not exist in your area.

ISBN-13: 978-0-373-52832-5

THE CROWN AFFAIR

First North American Publication 2011

This edition published by arrangement with Harlequin Books S.A.

For questions and comments about the quality of this book please contact us at Customer_eCare@Harlequin.ca.

www.Harlequin.com

Printed in U.S.A.

THE CROWN AFFAIR

To my parents

CHAPTER ONE

'Oh. My. God,' Laura muttered, her fingers tightening around her binoculars and her breath hitching in her throat at the sight that met her eyes.

Her heart skipped a beat and her entire body flushed with a heat that had nothing to do with the warmth of the early summer sun and everything to do with the view.

Because, wow, what a view…

There, approximately two hundred metres away, across a lush green field and over a drystone wall, in one corner of the extensive grounds of the manor house, was a man.

Standing with his back to her, bending down and hauling a hefty log onto a stump. Wearing nothing but a pair of jeans, heavy-duty work boots and a rather impressive tan.

Whoever he was, he was dark-haired and tall. Broad-shouldered and fit. The muscles of his shoulders and back twisted and flexed as he hammered the axe down on those poor helpless little logs, displaying such strength and control that every inch of her began to tingle.

When he moved round the other side of the stump and lifted the axe high above his head, the tingle turned to full-blown lust. For a brief frozen moment, in sharp definition, there was the most magnificent chest she'd ever seen. Tanned. Lean. Sprinkled with a smattering of dark hair that narrowed down his taut stomach and vanished tantalisingly beneath the waistband of his jeans.

Ignoring the little voice in her head telling her she really ought not to be doing this, Laura pressed the binoculars closer and bit her lip, largely to stop herself whimpering.

She'd never whimpered in her life, but if ever there was an occasion to start, this was it.

She could make out every rippling muscle. Every one of his ribs. Her fingers itched to trace the dips and contours of his body. What would he feel like beneath her hands? What would it feel like to have all that strength and control on top of her? Underneath her? Inside her?

At the bolt of desire that burst deep inside her, Laura's temperature went through the roof. The breath shot from her lungs and her heart practically stopped. A weird kind of fizzing sprang to life in the pit of her stomach and she clutched at the curtain before her balance vaporised and she nearly toppled out of the window.

Good Lord, she thought dazedly as stars spun around her head. She was fantasising. Ogling. Virtually salivating. Since when had she started doing *that*? She dragged in a shaky breath. Crikey, maybe she really *had* gone off the rails.

Letting the binoculars dangle from the leather strap hanging around her neck, Laura sagged against the wall and willed her breathing to steady and her heart rate to slow.

Now, of all times, when she was by herself and inches from an open window with a ten-foot drop to the ground, would really *not* be a good time to faint.

Which was precisely why she ought to unwrap herself from the curtains, back away and pull herself together.

Besides, quite apart from her precarious position, she had no business ogling men, however hot. After the traumatic collapse of her last relationship she'd sworn off the whole lousy lot of them. And even if she had been in the mood, voyeurism had never been her thing. It was sneaky. It was reckless.

And kind of thrilling.

Laura swallowed and blinked to clear her suddenly blurry vision. Oh, for heaven's sake. That little thrill currently whooshing around her body could stop it right now. She was interested in the house, that was all.

For the six weeks she'd been living in the village the manor house had been as silent as the grave, and her frustration at not being able to take a look inside had reached such a peak that if she weren't such a law-abiding person she'd have contemplated a spot of breaking and entering.

So when she'd heard the sound of splintering wood coming from the other side of the village earlier this morning she'd barely been able to believe her luck. Grabbing her binoculars, she'd raced upstairs, wrapped herself in her curtains and scouted the landscape for the source of the noise.

Quite what she'd been expecting she wasn't sure, but it certainly hadn't been a sight as enticing as this.

As the thrill returned, more delicious and more insistent than before, Laura paused mid-unwrap, nibbled on her lip and frowned. She'd always appreciated beauty. Had always admired structure. Which was why she'd become an architect. Now here was the finest animate example of both she'd seen in a long time and given the current sorry state of her love life it was unlikely that she'd ever get the chance again.

Her heart thumping with illicit excitement, she edged closer to the wall, huddled deeper into the curtain, and fished her binoculars out from beneath the heavy fabric.

How could another second or two hurt? After all, it wasn't as if he could see her, was it?

Matt swung the axe high above his head and froze.

There it was again. The flash.

Once. Twice. And then intermittently, like a sputtering light bulb. Like a beacon. Or like the sun glinting off a pair of binoculars.

Hell.

He thwacked the axe down on the log with such force that the blade scythed through the wood like a hot knife through butter and lodged in the stump.

Something hard and tight settled in the pit of his stomach. Couldn't they leave him alone for *one* measly second?

Ignoring the stinging in his muscles and the sweat trickling down his back, he bent down, picked up the two halves of the log and hurled them onto the pile.

One last weekend of peace. That was all he wanted. One lousy weekend of privacy before he embarked on a role he wasn't sure he was entirely prepared for, and life as he knew it turned upside down.

Matt grabbed the bottle lying in the grass, sloshed water over his head and flinched when the ice-cold liquid hit his burning skin.

Hadn't he provided the press with enough stories recently? They'd been hounding him for weeks, ever since it had been announced he was the long-lost heir to the newly restored Sassanian throne. They'd been camping outside his London house and tailing him wherever he went. Shoving tape recorders and cameras in his face at every opportunity and demanding responses to questions about his private life he had no intention of ever answering.

By and large he'd played his part. Given interviews. Posed for photographs. And borne it with remarkable, if grim, tolerance. But by following him here, to the house in the Cotswolds he'd almost forgotten he owned, they'd crossed the line.

As irritation escalated into anger, Matt shoved his hands through his hair and pulled his T-shirt over his head.

Enough was enough. No way was he just sitting back and letting some miserable lowlife hack gawk at him all weekend. To hell with the consequences. He was going to go round, grab that pair of binoculars and wind the strap round their scrawny neck.

Ah, that was a shame, thought Laura, biting her lip as she watched that magnificent chest disappear beneath a swathe of navy cotton.

If she had control of the world, a man like that would be consigned to a life of naked-from-the-waist-up log-chopping. On permanent display. As a gift to the nation or something. And if she had control of the world, she'd rewind time and hit the pause button at the exact moment he'd taken that impromptu little shower.

Despite the heat simmering in her veins, Laura shivered as the image slammed into her head. Utterly transfixed, she'd followed the rivulets of water trickling down his chest and hadn't been able to stop herself trembling with longing. The powerful lenses of her binoculars had picked out every glistening drop clinging lovingly to his skin and her breath had evaporated all over again.

Even now, when he was all covered up and striding across the lawn towards the house, as if the hounds of hell were snapping at his heels, she felt as if she were on fire. Tiny flames of heat licked along her veins. Her skin sizzled. Her stomach churned.

He disappeared inside the house and Laura blinked and felt a sharp pang of loss.

The unsettling shock of such an intense reaction snapped her back to her senses. She blinked. Rubbed her eyes and pulled herself together.

Right, she decided, unwinding herself from the curtain and setting the binoculars on her dressing table. That was quite enough of that. She'd indulged for far longer than was wise and she had things to do.

So no more thumping hearts and trembling limbs. No more tingling in inappropriate places and erratic breathing. And definitely no more fantasising.

Tucking a notebook and pencil in the back pocket of her shorts and slinging her camera over her shoulder, Laura pulled her shoulders back and headed downstairs.

If she was going to wangle an invitation inside what appeared to be a near perfect example of early seventeenth century architecture, she had to be charming, determined and above all, strong of knee.

One of the first things Matt had planned to do once installed on the throne of Sassania was open up the press and grant the country's journalists more access to information.

Now, he thought grimly, eyes down as he strode along the path in the direction of the binocular-toting hack, he wasn't so sure. Now he'd like to abolish it altogether and string up the entire lot of them. Starting with the one he was about to tear a strip off.

'Good morning.'

At the sound of the voice a few feet in front of him, Matt skidded to a halt and his head snapped up. His gaze rested on the woman blocking his path smiling blindingly at him and for a second his mind went blank. All thoughts of journalists and Mediterranean island kingdoms evaporated; if someone had asked his name he'd have been stumped.

As his gaze automatically ran over her he felt the ground tilt beneath his feet. Blood roared in his ears and fire surged through his veins. His chest contracted as if he'd been walloped in the solar plexus, and for one horrible moment Matt wondered if he was having a heart attack.

But then as suddenly as it had started, it stopped. The ground settled, his head cleared, his lungs started pumping and his heart rate steadied.

Keeping his extraordinary reaction firmly behind the neutral expression that had helped him make billions, Matt shoved a hand through his hair and forced himself to relax.

No doubt it was the unexpectedness of her that had caused his violent reaction. The sudden interruption to his train of thought. That was all. It couldn't possibly have had anything to do with the mass of blond hair, the big cornflower-blue eyes or the wide smile. Or, for that matter, the set of killer curves encased in the skimpiest shorts and tightest T-shirt he'd ever seen.

Because that would be as disconcerting as it would have been unusual. He'd never been distracted by a woman, however beautiful and however well packaged, and he didn't intend to start now.

Reminding himself what he was supposed to be doing, he gave her a brief nod and the flash of an impersonal smile. 'Good morning,' he said, taking a step to the right to weave past her.

Which she mirrored.

Matt frowned. 'Excuse me,' he muttered, and took a step to the left.

Which she blocked, too.

He rubbed a hand along his jaw and stifled a sigh. Once might have been an accident. Twice was deliberate.

Matt bit back a growl of frustration. This was precisely why up until now he'd chosen to live in a penthouse in an exclusive apartment block in the centre of London, where none of the neighbours knew each other and no one was interested in wasting time on idle chitchat. Everyone kept themselves to themselves and just got on with their own lives.

Here, however, out in the country, things evidently didn't work like that. Whoever she was, she clearly wanted to chat. While he didn't. Nor did he have the time to tango from side to side like this all morning.

Toying with the idea of clamping his hands round her waist and hoisting her out of the way, Matt dipped his eyes to the narrow strip of bare flesh between the hem of her T-shirt and the waistband of her shorts.

He wondered what it would feel like. Smooth. Silky. Warm. Undoubtedly. And what would it taste like? At the thought of his mouth against the skin of her stomach, moving lower and lower to see what *she'd* taste like, his mouth went dry and his pulse leapt.

Hmm, he thought, shoving his fists in his pockets.

Perhaps putting his hands on her wasn't the wisest course of action. Conversation, polite but brief, it would have to be. Assuming he could speak, of course.

'Are you all right?' she asked, her brow creasing in concern.

Matt gave his head a quick shake to dispel the lingering fuzziness and cleared his throat. 'Fine,' he said. 'Why?'

'You went very pale for a second.'

'You startled me.'

Her smiled widened and his temperature went up a notch. 'I'm sorry,' she said. 'I thought it would be safer to alert you to my presence rather than wait for you to barrel straight into me.'

At the thought of his body colliding with hers, of having all that softness and warmth plastered against him, a bolt of desire kicked him in the gut. A vision of the two of them tumbling down onto the grass, limbs entwined, mouths jammed together, hands everywhere, slammed into his head and his heart nearly leapt out of his chest.

So much for trying to kid himself that his reaction to her was simply shock. Shock had never given him an erection harder than granite.

Great. Scorching attraction. Just what he needed.

Matt's jaw tightened. 'I was deep in thought,' he said, finally drumming up some of that steely control he was supposedly so famous for and hauling his body into line.

She tilted her head to one side. 'I could tell. And not about anything good by the looks of things.'

'Not particularly.'

'That's a shame.'

'Is it?'

She nibbled on her lip and nodded. 'I think so. Especially on a day like today.'

'What's so special about today?' Apart from being the day he thought he might be losing his mind.

'Well, for one thing, the sun is shining, and, this being Britain in May, that's a cause for celebration. Plus the flowers are beautiful and the air smells heavenly.'

Were they? Did it? Matt had been too wrapped up in his thoughts to notice. Now his thoughts had been scattered to the four winds. Forget the flowers. Forget the air. *She* was beautiful. *She* smelt heavenly. And her mouth was something else. 'Really?' he muttered, trying not to imagine what it would feel like crushed beneath his.

She nodded. 'A day like today should be all about lying on the grass, reading the papers and drinking rosé,' she said, giving him another wide smile that had his control threatening to unravel all over again, 'not marching around and glowering at the ground.'

At that timely reminder about where he was and what he was supposed to be doing, Matt pulled himself together. This was ludicrous. If the people of Sassania could see the state of him now, they'd have thought twice about their decision to reinstate the monarchy.

'Unfortunately I don't have time to read the papers or drink rosé,' he said sharply. And as for sprawling over the grass, well, the less he thought about that the better. 'So, if you'll excuse me...'

She stuck out her hand. 'Laura Mackenzie.'

Matt resisted the urge to grind his teeth. 'Matt Saxon.' He took her hand and ignored the leap of electricity that shot up his arm. 'Look, is there something I can help you with?'

'I hope so.' Her voice sounded a little hoarse and she ran her hand over her hip as she cleared her throat.

Matt frowned. 'If it's directions you're after I'm afraid I won't be of much use.' He spent so little time in the area he'd had to programme his satnav just to get here.

She shook her head and the sun bouncing off her hair, dazzled him for a second. 'I'm not after directions.' She shot him another smile that made his stomach contract. 'In fact I'm after you.'

For a second Matt couldn't work out what she was talking about. 'Me?'

She nodded and a chill, as if the sun had disappeared behind a cloud, snaked down his spine. The lingering trace of desire fled and his body tightened for an entirely different reason.

Why would she be after him? How did she know who he was?

Unless she'd been watching him.

As suspicion slammed into him his pulse began to race. She couldn't be...

He ran his gaze over her again, this time skating over the curves and the clothing. This time his eyes clocked the camera slung over her shoulder. The corner of a notebook and the pen sticking out of the back pocket of her shorts. The hopeful, eager look on her face.

The chill running through his body turned to ice. Oh, damn. It appeared she was.

His gaze trailed back up and he scrutinised her features, comparing them against the bank of journalistic faces he'd filed away over the past few months. But he drew a blank. Whoever she worked for, he thought grimly, she was new.

Stamping down hard on something that felt suspiciously like disappointment, Matt hardened his heart. Why was he surprised? Why was he disappointed? Once again life was simply proving that some people were only out for what they could get.

'I'm glad we bumped into each other,' she said.

He just bet she was. 'Why?'

The smile faltered and her eyes widened a fraction at his tone. 'I was on my way to see you.'

'Were you?' he drawled as a strange sort of numbness seeped through him.

'You've come from the manor house.'

'I have.'

Matt shoved his hands in the pockets of his jeans and rocked back on his heels, deciding to wait and see to what lengths this one would go to wangle an interview. Her outfit was certainly designed to kill.

'Nice place.'

'Thank you,' he said coolly.

'Fabulous detail on the gabling.'

'Really.'

'Absolutely. And beautiful—er—grounds.'

'Naturally.'

'Are you the gardener?'

Matt frowned. The gardener? Hah. 'I'm the owner.' As if she didn't know.

Her eyes widened. 'Oh.' And then she gave him a smile that had the ground beneath his feet tilting all over again before he could tell it not to. 'Well, that's even better.'

'Of course it is.'

She frowned and blinked. 'What?'

Oh, she did the innocent thing very well. 'What do you want?' he said.

Laura's smile faltered. 'If it's not too much trouble,

I was wondering if I could come over and take some photos. Of your house,' she added.

Too much trouble? Matt's jaw clenched. The complete and utter gall of the woman.

'It would only be for a second,' she added, as if sensing his reluctance. 'You know, just a few shots. If you wouldn't mind...'

Matt's tenuous grip on his patience snapped. 'Yes, I do mind, and no, you can't.'

The smile slid from her face and she recoiled as if he'd slapped her. For a moment she just stood there, staring at him in shock, her face draining of colour so fast he thought she might be about to pass out.

Matt steeled himself against the brief stab of guilt and the flash of distress in her eyes and told himself not to be so idiotically soft.

What the hell had she expected? That he'd welcome her into his house with open arms? That he'd *want* to be photographed lounging on the sofa in his drawing room? That he'd roll over and offer her a double-page spread of the new ruler of Sassania 'at home'?

If she really thought that, she could think again.

Laura blinked a couple of times and then pulled her shoulders back. 'Oh. Right,' she said blankly. 'Well. Sorry to have bothered you. Enjoy your weekend.'

Like that was a possibility now.

As she gave him a vague nod and turned to walk back in the direction she had presumably come from, Matt's hand shot out and clamped around her upper arm. 'Not so fast.'

CHAPTER TWO

WHAT the hell?

Laura felt Matt's fingers dig into her arm and went rigid as alarm flooded through her.

Well, alarm and a whole lot of something else. But alarm was what she decided to channel at that particular moment. Because he might have eyes the colour of dark molten chocolate and thick brown hair that her fingers itched to thread through. He might have a voice that made her think of whisky and honey and warm nights in front of a fire. And he might have a body that she longed to get her hands on.

But he was clearly a psychopath.

All she'd wanted was a bit of a snoop and a few lousy shots of his house, for goodness' sake. Anyone would think she'd been after his soul.

'Ow,' she muttered, wincing and trying to wriggle away from beneath his fingers.

His grip loosened and she pulled back and rubbed her arm where her skin burned. If she had any sense whatsoever she'd be spinning on her heel and racing back to the safety of her cottage. For although she'd been drooling over his house for weeks, at no point had she considered the fact that its owner would be anything other than congenial and cooperative.

Hah. How wrong could you get?

Laura glanced up to find him glowering at her and nearly swooned at the fierceness of his glare. Whatever his problem was, and he clearly had many, she wanted nothing to do with it. She had enough problems of her own. The biggest one at the moment being the treacherous way her body appeared to respond to him.

When he'd taken her hand she'd nearly leapt a foot in the air from the jolt of electricity that shot up her arm. And then when he'd looked her up and down, so thoroughly, as if he could see right through her clothes, every inch of her body had burned in the wake of his gaze. The heat that had whipped through her when she'd been ogling him through her binoculars had been nothing compared to the scorching heat that was thundering through her now.

In the face of such blatant hostility her reaction to him was perverse.

What exactly was it about that penetrating stare of his that pinned her to the spot? Why were her insides going all squirmy and quivery? And more importantly, why wasn't she taking advantage of the fact that he'd released her, and running off just as fast as her size sevens would carry her?

That was what the old Laura, the one who avoided confrontation like the plague and never said no, would have done. And despite the assertiveness course she'd recently completed, there was enough of the old her still floating around to make her long to run and bury herself under her duvet.

But scarpering in the face of confrontation wasn't an option any longer, was it? Laura squared her jaw. No. Now she dealt with stuff. Or at least that was the idea. Up until now she hadn't had the opportunity to practise.

Channelling everything she could remember from the course, Laura took a deep breath, stuck her chin up and returned his glare. 'What do you want now?'

'Who do you work for?' he snapped.

She blinked and inwardly flinched. 'That's none of your business.'

'What?' His eyebrows shot up.

Laura bristled. 'Well, who do you think you are hauling me around and demanding to know who I work for?' She tilted her head and shot him a defiant stare. Her tutor would be proud. 'You know, your small-talk skills leave a *lot* to be desired.'

Matt's face tightened. 'I'm not interested in small talk. Do you or do you not work for *Celebrity* magazine?'

Laura frowned. Maybe the mushrooms she'd eaten for breakfast had had a touch of the magic about them, because this conversation had her baffled. 'Of course I don't. Currently I don't work for anyone.'

'Freelance?' he snapped.

Made redundant, but there was no way she was going into that. 'On sabbatical.'

'Right,' he drawled, clearly not believing her for a second. 'Then why were you watching me?'

Uh-oh. Laura's mouth opened. Then closed. And then to her dismay she felt her cheeks begin to burn. 'What makes you think anyone was watching you?' she said, aiming for a blank look in the hope that it would counteract the blush. If asked, she'd attribute *that* to the heat.

Matt raised an eyebrow. 'Well, let me see,' he said dryly. 'How about a pair of binoculars glinting in the sun and pointing straight in my direction?'

Oh, rats. Laura's heart plummeted. So much for thinking she'd been discreet. She shouldn't have pushed her luck and indulged for so long.

Her brain raced through her options and she realised depressingly that she had no choice but to confess. Since she'd already told him she'd come looking for him she couldn't even bluff her way out of it.

She ran a hand through her hair and straightened her spine. 'OK, fine. But technically I wasn't actually—'

'I'll ask you one more time,' he said flatly, his eyes narrowing. 'Which scurrilous rag do you work for?'

Which scurrilous rag? Laura's hand fell to her side and she blinked in confusion. What on earth was he talking about? Perhaps she ought to suggest he get out of the heat. What with all that bending and twisting while log-chopping, the sun must have gone to his head. Something had certainly gone to hers and she hadn't even been in the sun. 'I don't work for a rag, scurrilous or otherwise,' she said. 'I'm an architect.'

A flicker of surprise flashed across his face and then vanished. 'That's one I haven't heard before.'

Laura's hackles shot up. 'It's not a joke.'

'You're absolutely right.'

'Why would you think I was a journalist?'

'I don't think, I *know* you're a journalist.'

Her mouth dropped open at the scorn in his voice and she had to dig deep and drum up the techniques to Embrace Confrontation to fight back the temptation to quail. 'You're insane.'

A muscle in his jaw hammered. 'So explain the binoculars.'

Laura planted her hands on her hips and glared at him. 'I was about to when you interrupted me.'

Matt's expression took on a 'this'll be good' kind of

look and indignation simmered in her veins. Why the hell was she bothering? Oh, yes, the house.

Laura tightened her grip on her manners. 'I was going to clarify that I wasn't actually watching you.' Much. 'I was really eyeing up your house.'

He stared at her. 'My house?' he said, his brows snapping together. 'Why?'

'Because it's the best example of seventeenth century architecture I've ever seen. Certainly round here.'

'That's not uncommon knowledge,' he drawled.

Laura couldn't help bristling at his sceptical tone. 'Undoubtedly,' she said tightly. 'However I have more than a passing interest. I specialise in the restoration and conservation of ancient buildings, and I've been coveting yours for weeks.'

'Is that so?'

Matt folded his arms across his chest and stared at her. For so long and so intently that she began to drown in the heat of his gaze. She might be churning with indignation, but that didn't stop her head swimming, her knees turning watery and her stomach fluttering. Laura silently cursed her treacherous body and hoped to God he couldn't see the effect he was having on her. 'Absolutely,' she said with a coolness that came from who knew where.

Matt tilted his head. Raised an eyebrow. Gave her a lazily lethal smile that zoomed down the entire length of her body and curled her toes, and quite suddenly her skin began to prickle.

'If you're an architect as you say you are,' he said, leaning forwards a fraction and lowering his voice, 'prove it.'

Prove it? *Prove it?*

For a moment, all Laura could hear was what sounded

like the faint hum of a tractor somewhere in the distance. But that could well have been the blood rushing in her ears.

'What?' she said, giving her head a quick shake. Presumably she'd been so distracted by the muscles of Matt's arms flexing as he crossed them she must have misheard. Been hypnotised by his eyes or something. Or maybe he just had a truly warped sense of humour and was joking. Because what kind of man went round accusing random strangers of being something they weren't and then demanding they prove it?

'If you expect me to believe you're an architect and want nothing more than access to my house, prove it.'

Laura blinked and stared at him. Nope. Gorgeous forearms and mesmerising eyes aside, she hadn't misheard. And he wasn't joking. That he meant what he said was etched into the stony expression on his face.

Her pulse raced. What exactly was his problem? Was he on some sort of lord-of-the-manor power trip? Was he completely paranoid? And frankly, did she even want to venture inside his house when he was obviously one pane short of a window?

The rational side of her, the one that was seething with indignation, pointed out that she had no need to continue this idiotic conversation. It was a balmy Saturday morning. She had plenty of things to be getting on with. Like finding a job and sorting out her catastrophe of a life. She really didn't need this kind of headache, and no mansion was worth this amount of hassle.

However, the professional part of her, the one that had recently been so ruthlessly dismissed, so flatly rejected by the company she'd worked for, clamoured for the opportunity to justify her abilities.

The two sides battled for a nanosecond but the sting of rejection was still so fresh, the wound still so raw, there was no contest.

Laura pulled her shoulders back and stuck her chin up. He wanted proof? Then he'd get it. More of it than anyone not fascinated with old buildings could possibly want.

'Fine,' she said, hauling out her notebook and studying the notes she'd made over the past six weeks. 'From my preliminary investigations I'd say your house was probably built some time between the late sixteenth and early seventeenth centuries. The main structure has two storeys and, I believe, an attic.'

Possibly with a mad relative in occupancy to accompany the one who inhabited the rest.

'It's built out of squared and dressed limestone,' she continued, 'and has a stone slate roof. I believe it used to be a quadrangle, but it's now "h" shaped with wings projecting forwards right and left of the central gabled porch. The right hand wing has been substantially rebuilt at the back. I'd say in the mid-nineteenth century.'

She paused to take a breath and glanced up from the pages to find Matt staring at her, a slightly stunned expression on his handsome face.

Good. That would teach him to leap to absurd conclusions and engage in all that sceptical eyebrow raising. And she had plenty more where that came from. She hadn't even begun on the windows.

She arched a challenging eyebrow of her own. 'Would you like me to go on?'

Matt frowned. 'No. That's fine.'

Stuffing the notebook back in her pocket, Laura pulled her camera off her shoulder and switched it on. 'Then perhaps you'd like to see some pictures?' she said.

'I have one hundred and thirty photos of Regency Bath. I could take you through each one of them if you like. In great detail. I'm very thorough. And extremely enthusiastic. Honestly I could talk about them for hours.'

The frown deepened. 'Some other time perhaps. I'm convinced.'

Bully for him. 'I'm so glad,' she said witheringly, hauling her camera back on her shoulder and shooting him a cool glance. 'So why would you think I was a journalist?'

'Experience of binoculars.'

'Are you really that newsworthy?'

His mouth twisted into a wry smile. 'I have been.'

She racked her brains to place his face, but drew a blank. He probably dated supermodels or something. Poor old supermodels. 'Who are you?'

'Ever read the papers?'

Laura shook her head. 'Not often. Too much doom and gloom. Unless you've appeared in *Architecture Tomorrow*, I'm unlikely to have heard of you.' So there.

'How refreshing.'

Now she was naïve as well as everything else? Wow, he really knew how to make women feel special.

'How patronising,' she fired back, before she could remind herself that he still held all the cards and she was supposed to be being charming and polite.

Matt didn't say anything. Just looked at her steadily with those dark eyes of his until the urge to kick herself became almost impossible to contain.

Rats. Had she gone too far? Been *too* demanding, and blown it? Laura caught her lip and frowned. Damn, that assertiveness course had a lot to answer for.

Then the glimmer of a smile hovered at his mouth

and the tension that she hadn't realised she'd been feeling fled her body. 'It appears I owe you an apology.'

Phew. Thank God for that. She hadn't blown it. 'It *appears* you owe me an apology?' she said, her eyebrows lifting a fraction as she gave him a broad smile.

He shrugged and shoved his hands in his pockets. 'More than one probably. You'll have to bear with me, though, I'm a little rusty.'

That was the understatement of the century. 'An apology would be good,' Laura said, deciding to capitalise on his obvious unease and press home her advantage. 'An invitation to take a look around your house would be better.'

Invite her to take a look round his house?

The faint smile tugging at Matt's lips vanished.

That was absolutely out of the question.

Apart from the invasion of his privacy, with his judgement so skewed and his behaviour so unpredictable, who knew what might happen once she was inside his house and within stumbling distance of a bed?

Matt frowned as his mind raced. He was usually so measured. So careful in his decisions. He never went off the rails. Never made mistakes. So why now?

Maybe the memories the house held were more unsettling than he'd thought. Maybe the stress of the past six months had got too much. Maybe he was cracking up.

Because why else would he have leapt to the wrong conclusion and rushed over here? Why else would he have completely overreacted and lashed out at her? And why else would he be finding it so hard to keep his hands off her?

The flush of colour in her cheeks, the flashing of her

eyes and the heaving of her breasts made him want to behave in the kind of prehistoric way that he doubted would go down well with a twenty-first-century woman. Even when he'd thought she was a journalist and had been burning with fury, he'd still wanted to throw her over his shoulder and cart her off to the nearest bedroom.

Which was never going to happen. Even if he'd wanted to explore the attraction that sizzled between them he didn't have the time and really didn't need the complication.

Ignoring the sliver of regret that pierced his chest, Matt set his jaw and pulled himself together. A tower of strength, that was him. Rock hard. Implacable.

Above all, he was absolutely not cracking up and it was about time he proved it. Giving Laura a polite smile, he hardened his heart. 'I'm afraid that's completely out of the question.'

Oh.

Laura's smile faded and her shoulders sagged a little at Matt's flatly delivered response. A flood of disappointment washed through her and a lump formed in her throat. Dammit, she could have sworn he'd been about to agree to her request. She'd thought she'd had it so in the bag.

But as she stared up at him, taking in the rigid expression on his face and his unyielding stance, it was blindingly obvious that Matt had made his decision, and it was equally clear that nothing she said would make him change his mind. He looked unforgiving, unbending and as immovable as granite.

She swallowed back the lump and inwardly shrugged. Ah, well. She'd tried. That was the main thing.

She'd given it her best shot and been defeated. Matt clearly valued his privacy and definitely wanted to be left alone. He'd made his decision and she'd respect that. So her curiosity would remain unsatisfied, but that didn't matter. There were plenty of other equally interesting houses she could visit if she felt like it. It really was no big deal.

She was on the point of turning on her heel and leaving when her conscience suddenly decided to wake up and demand to know what the hell she thought she was doing.

Hang on a minute. She froze as her head began to pound. Was she really going to give in just like that? After all she'd been through? After all the self-analysis she'd done? After all the money and energy she'd spent on that course?

What was she? A wimp or a warrior?

Feeling determination begin to course through her, Laura stiffened her resolve. Hadn't she vowed to banish her inner wimp and embrace her inner warrior?

She had. At length. So no way was she going to let the wimp win.

This wasn't about the house any more. This was about her, and the promise she'd made to herself to shuck off the old Laura and embrace the new.

Matt might be standing there like Everest, but he was still a man, flesh and blood just like anyone else. Well, not *quite* like anyone else, she thought, letting her gaze roam over him and feeling her temperature rocket, but he was bound to have an Achilles heel somewhere. All she had to do was find it.

She'd get what she came for. By whatever means possible.

* * *

Why wasn't she spinning on her heel and going?

Matt watched the emotions play across Laura's face and his frown deepened. He'd made it perfectly clear his answer was no, so why was she still hovering there?

More to the point, why was *he* still hovering there? Just because she was running her gaze over him didn't mean he had to stay until she'd finished, did it?

'Oh,' she said, her teeth catching on her lower lip as she finally lifted her face and batted her eyelids up at him.

Oh, no, Matt thought, steeling himself against the nugget of guilt that suddenly started tugging at his conscience. He was *not* going to be swayed by the disappointment swimming in the big blue eyes shimmering up at him. Or distracted by the wet red pout of her mouth.

No way. The guilt and the desire could get lost. He pulled his hands out of his pockets and dragged them through his hair. Dammit, this was precisely why he should have been the one to leave.

'Please,' she said, looking up at him from beneath her lashes, the pout curving into an enticing smile.

Matt's gaze dropped to her mouth before he could stop it and he was thwacked by a vision of those lips roaming over his body, her hair fanning out and tickling his skin as she moved down him, her hands stroking everywhere. At the force of the desire that slammed through him his mouth went dry and his head swam.

And for the life of him he couldn't remember why letting her loose in his house was a bad idea.

'OK,' he heard himself say. 'Sure. Why not?'

'Great,' she said, the disappointment vanishing from her eyes and her smile switching from enticing to strangely triumphant. 'Lead the way.'

Why not? *Why not?* God. He was definitely cracking up. Wishing he could give himself a good slap, Matt muttered a 'Follow me,' turned on his heel and marched off.

CHAPTER THREE

WELL, that had been something of a surprise, thought Laura, resisting the urge to punch the air and setting off in Matt's wake instead. Having never employed such wily tactics before, she hadn't really expected the pout and the eyelash flutter to work. But while she might be faintly stunned that they had, Matt, judging by the merciless pace he set as he stalked along the path, was fuming.

By the time they reached the front door of the house Laura was hot, panting and, without doubt, hideously red in the face. Matt, on the other hand, hadn't broken a sweat.

If she was being brutally honest, her current breathlessness wasn't *entirely* due to the unexpected exercise. She'd trotted along behind him, her gaze fixed to his lithe muscular frame as if magnetised, and her body had begun to hum with something other than adrenalin. The easy way he moved and the purposefulness of his stride had her thinking about all the other things he might do purposefully and easily, and her head had gone all fuzzy. She'd scraped her hair back into a messy ponytail in the faint hope it might cool her down but it hadn't worked.

'Where would you like to start?' he snapped, dropping his keys onto the console table and whipping round to face her.

With the removal of his T-shirt ideally, Laura decided, totally distracted by the rippling muscles in his forearms as he crossed them over his chest. First she'd slide her hands beneath it and draw it over his head. Once she'd dealt with that she'd run her hands down his torso and tackle his belt. Then she'd undo the buttons of his jeans, hook her hands over the waistband and ease them down over his hips before pushing him down onto a deep soft sofa that was bound to be lurking somewhere around the place. And then she'd sink to her knees and—

'Laura?'

Laura blinked and hurtled back to reality. God. She was doing it again. At the heat that rushed through her, her cheeks began to burn even more fiercely.

For the first time since she'd decided to become an architect she thanked God for the eighteenth century window tax that had bricked up thousands of windows and ultimately led to dark halls across the country. Including, to her eternal gratitude, this one.

'Yes. Sorry.' She blinked and swallowed and gathered her scattered wits. The house. He was talking about the house. Of course. 'The—ah—attic, I think,' she said. As far away from Matt and his disturbing effect on her equilibrium as possible.

'I'll take you to it,' he said, heading for the stairs.

What? Alarm knotted her stomach. He was planning to accompany her? Laura shivered at the thought. With him watching her every move she'd never get anything done.

'No,' she blurted out.

Matt stopped, turned and stared at her in surprise. As well he might.

'I mean, it's fine,' she added hastily with a quick smile. 'I'm sure you have things to be getting on with and I should be able to find the attic. Top of the house, right?'

'Where else?'

He stared at her, his eyes narrowing as if trying to work out if she was entirely trustworthy, and, what with the unorthodox methods she'd employed to inveigle her way inside his house, she couldn't entirely blame him.

'Well, quite.' Laura swallowed hard and tucked a tendril of hair behind her ear. 'Look, Matt,' she said, giving him what she hoped was a reassuring smile, 'I really do work better alone. And I promise not to run off with the silver.'

Matt frowned and then shrugged. 'Fine. I'll be in the library if you need anything.'

Oh, for God's sake, Matt thought, scowling down at the report into Sassania's fishing quotas that he'd been trying to work on and shoving it aside. How long did getting a few photos take? The house wasn't that big, but Laura had been up there for an hour at least. She couldn't have found *that* much of architectural interest, could she?

Something banged right above his head and Matt winced. Perhaps she had. Judging by the sounds of scraping furniture and the hammering on walls that had been coming from various parts of the house, Laura was taking the whole place apart.

While part of him reluctantly admired her thoroughness and determination, another, more persistent part of him had spent the past hour wondering whether her enthusiasm and passion for her work carried over into other areas of life. Like sex.

An image of her lying on his bed, naked, her hair spilling all over his pillows, her long tanned limbs tangled in his sheets, her eyes all slumberous and inviting, slammed into his head yet again and his body stiffened painfully.

Matt shoved his hands through his hair and ground his teeth in frustration. This was ridiculous. He was a sensible rational man of thirty-three, not a hormone-ridden adolescent. So why was he finding it so hard to concentrate? Why had he spent the past ten minutes reading the same page of that damned report with still no idea of what it was about?

It hadn't been *that* long since he'd had sex, had it? He cast his mind back and tried to remember the last time he'd had a woman in his bed. Was it six months ago? A year? Surely it couldn't be longer than that, could it?

Matt frowned. Even if it was, there was no need to panic. He'd been busy. That was all. And it wasn't as if he *needed* sex. He'd gone far longer without it and had survived perfectly well.

Footsteps echoed down the stairs. His blood rushed to his head and he pushed himself away from his desk and leapt to his feet. He needed to get out, before he did something really rash like bundle her back upstairs and demand she show him the architectural features of his bedroom.

He'd go and chop what was left of those logs. The release of hard physical work after spending months in stifling meeting rooms had worked earlier. It would work now. Just to be on the safe side he'd stay out there until she'd finished. If he ran out of logs, he'd fire up the lawnmower.

And there was another benefit of his strategy, he thought, identifying the sound of a camera clicking coming from the drawing room and striding across the hall. Laura could let herself out. Once he'd told her where he was going he need never lay eyes on her ever again. And then maybe, just maybe, his body would stop twitching and aching and straining, and he'd regain some sort of equilibrium.

Good. Excellent. It was a brilliant plan. With every step he took he could feel his head clearing and his sanity returning.

Until he got to the doorway. Where he stopped dead.

As he'd figured, Laura was in the drawing room. What he hadn't allowed for was that she'd be investigating the fireplace. With her back to him, on her knees. With her legs spread and her bottom in the air.

His gaze dropped, automatically zooming in on her bottom, and as his blood rushed to his feet and his body began to pound with lust the breath whooshed from his lungs and his brilliant plan turned to dust.

Laura sensed Matt's presence a nanosecond before she heard it. The nape of her neck pricked, her pulse skipped and goosebumps sprang up all over her skin. And then she caught the sharp exhalation of breath and the muttered oath, and with utter horror the picture she realised she must be presenting flashed into her head.

Barely a minute ago she'd walked into the drawing room and immediately spied the ornamented fireback of the fireplace. She'd rattled off a couple of photos before hunkering down to take a closer look. As a result she was on her hands and knees, face to the stone and bottom to the air.

Oh, God. A cold clammy sweat broke out over her entire body as mortification flooded through her. It was so not a good look. Heaven only knew what Matt must be thinking.

Desperately seeking to claw back some kind of dignity, Laura clambered to her feet as elegantly and quickly as she could.

Which would have been absolutely fine had she not been tucked inside a four-foot-high fireplace.

Realisation came way too late.

As did Matt's shout of warning.

With a sickening thud her skull cracked against solid seventeenth century stone. Her yelp of shock ricocheted around the fireplace. For a second she could feel absolutely nothing. Could see nothing but a fuzzy sort of blackness dotted with stars. Could hear nothing but the hammering of her heart.

Then as the blackness faded an excruciating pain shot the entire length of her body and spread throughout her limbs. She let out an agonised gasp. Her stomach churned and sent a wave of nausea rolling into her throat. Her knees buckled and she crumpled. She screwed her eyes tight shut and braced herself for more unimaginable pain.

Which didn't come.

How strange. Where was the agony? Where was the shock?

Faintly bewildered, Laura just hung there for a second, suspended by two bands of steel that had come from who knew where and snapped round her waist. Come to think of it, what exactly was the solid thing she was pressed up against and why was her body suddenly zinging with electricity?

Her heart beginning to pound even faster, Laura gingerly opened her eyes. And found herself staring straight up into Matt's, so close, so dark and so focused on her that she nearly saw stars all over again.

When he'd caught her he'd evidently had to clamp her to him. Now every inch of her body was plastered up against his and awareness fizzled along her nerve endings. She could feel the tension in his muscles as he held her. She could feel his heart banging against the palm of her hand. The intoxicating scent of him enveloped her, seeped into her head and made her dizzy.

He was so close she could see flecks of gold in the brown of his eyes. So close his mouth was barely an inch from her own. The lingering traces of pain and shock receded and slow drugging desire began to hum in the pit of her stomach.

Laura's pulse leapt. Her lips actually tingled. All she'd have to do would be to lift her head a fraction and she could put an end to the speculation and find out exactly what he tasted like. Perhaps she could blame it on concussion, because, Lord, it was tempting.

But it was also just not on, Laura reminded herself, dragging her gaze from Matt's mouth and fixing it firmly on the wedge of tanned flesh exposed by the V of his T-shirt.

The only reason she was in his house was because she'd guilt-tripped him into it. He didn't really want her here and, as was clear from the scowl on his face, he wasn't exactly ecstatic about having had to jump to her rescue.

A kiss from her would be about as welcome to him as UPVC windows were to her. No doubt about it.

Unfortunately knowing that wasn't apparently enough to stop a deep sigh of longing escaping her lips.

Heat rushed to her cheeks in the silence that followed.

God, she really hoped Matt hadn't caught that. And she really hoped he couldn't feel her swelling breasts and hardening nipples press against his chest.

But as his arms tightened around her any hope she might have had that he hadn't noticed her reaction to him evaporated. Her heart skipped a beat. Her eyes jerked up and met his just in time to catch something flaring in the brown depths. Barely a flash, but it was enough to set her heart galloping and her head spinning. And then she felt another part of his anatomy flaring and the bottom fell out of her stomach.

Oh, good Lord.

It wasn't just her. He felt it, too. Laura's heart thumped. Judging by the impressive evidence swelling against her hip, Matt was as attracted to her as she was to him. His head was moving forward. His eyes were darkening as they roamed over her face, lingering on her mouth before sweeping back up to meet hers.

For a split second delight shot through her and then quite suddenly panic elbowed the delight aside and thumped her squarely in the chest. Her nerves started to twist into a tangled mess.

Oh, God. If Matt did want her as much as she wanted him then she ought to leave. As soon as possible.

Because if he did make a move and kissed her, she'd never be able to resist. One thing would lead to another and another and another, and before she knew it she'd be back where she started, assertiveness course or no assertiveness course.

It would be even worse if he *didn't* kiss her. Because then the danger was that what with her highly unstable behaviour of late *she'd* be the one to make a move.

Either way the outcome would be a disaster of epic proportions.

So why wasn't she pushing him away? Why was she letting him get closer?

Time seemed to skid to a halt and Laura couldn't move. Matt's hand came up to cup her face and her skin burned as if he'd branded her. Anticipation thundered through her and her bones melted. When he slid his hand up and threaded his fingers through her hair Laura couldn't help lifting her face. Couldn't stop her breath hitching and her lips parting.

God, who cared if she couldn't resist? If this was wrong, why did it feel so right? Her gaze dropped to his mouth and her heart hammered. Desperation to taste him clawed at her insides and she had to bite on her lip to stop another whimper of need escaping.

'It doesn't look as if you need stitches,' he murmured, 'but you'll have quite a bump.'

What?

Laura froze. The whimper died in her throat. For a moment bewilderment besieged her brain. And then clarity dawned and she went scorchingly hot.

Agh. The bump on her head couldn't possibly be any bigger than the one she'd just had crashing back to reality.

What on earth was the matter with her? How could she have got it so wrong? Thank God Matt had drawn back before she'd lost patience and grasped the initiative.

At the thought of just how massive a fool she could have made of herself mortification roared through her and made her cheeks burn. God, was there *no* hope for her?

Suddenly desperate to get away, Laura wriggled in his arms and pushed against his chest. When his arms loosened she stepped back. And nearly collapsed all over again.

'Steady,' he said, putting his hands on her shoulders and keeping her upright.

Laura summoned strength to her watery limbs, shook herself free and forced herself to meet his gaze. 'Look,' she said with a calmness she really didn't feel. 'Thank you for catching me and everything, but you must be busy and I've imposed quite long enough. I think I should go.'

Ten minutes ago Matt would have been first in line to agree. Now, with lust ricocheting around him so violently it made his head spin, he wasn't so sure.

He could still feel Laura in his arms, all that warmth and softness crushed up against him. Her scent, something light and jasminey, was still floating around inside his head. The memory of the smoothness of her cheek beneath his palm and the silkiness of her hair winding round his fingers made his hands itch to touch her again.

When she'd looked up at him with those extraordinary eyes of hers, her mouth parting and her breathing shallow, practically inviting him to kiss her senseless, it had taken every ounce of control he possessed not to do exactly that. Quite apart from the fact that he'd decided he really couldn't go there, she'd just banged her head. She might well have concussion.

Matt gritted his teeth and fought back the desire to haul her into his arms. Maybe he'd banged his head, too. Maybe *he* had concussion. What else could be causing this pummelling urge to disregard his common sense, throw caution to the wind, drag her down to the sofa and sink himself inside her?

It would be utter madness. He was about to disappear off to another country. He could promise her nothing even if he'd wanted to.

But it would also be fantastic. Dynamite. It would certainly beat chopping logs the whole weekend. It *had* been too long since he'd had a woman in his bed and who knew when the opportunity would next arise? Who knew when he'd have the time?

Desire pounded through him and his control began to unravel.

'Matt?' she said with a sexy kind of breathiness that had him envisaging her saying his name in a whole lot of other ways.

At the images that spun through his head, the last vestiges of his resistance crumbled and Matt gave in. He wanted her. She wanted him. Why shouldn't they go for it and to hell with the consequences?

Ruthlessly ignoring the little voice inside his head demanding to know what on earth he thought he was doing, Matt tilted his head and gave her a slow smile. 'I think you should stay.'

CHAPTER FOUR

STAY?

Oh, goodness.

Laura hadn't thought it possible for her heart to beat more rapidly than it had when she'd been draped in his arms, but she'd been wrong. It was now galloping so fast she feared it might leap out of her chest.

The atmosphere had turned electric. Something about the way Matt was looking at her made every hair on her body leap to attention and quiver. The intensity of his gaze, the tension in his body and the smouldering smile… A lethally attractive combination that made her stomach lurch. God, if she wasn't careful she'd be in so much trouble.

'For what?'

Matt shrugged, but his eyes glittered with intent. 'Lunch. The afternoon. Whatever.'

Lunch she could do. The afternoon would probably be manageable, too. It was the whatever that concerned her.

'I can't,' she said a little hoarsely, and cleared her throat.

'Why not?'

'I have plans.' That sounded good.

'Cancel them.'

'No.' Excellent. Firm and uncompromising, that was the thing.

'Why not?'

'I'm on sabbatical.'

'From lunch?'

'From everything.'

'Why?'

No way was she spilling out all the details of her disaster of a life. 'I have my reasons.'

Matt's eyes darkened. 'I'm not suggesting you give up your sabbatical altogether. Just take a quick break.'

He ran his gaze over her and her body burned in the wake of its trail. Her breasts swelled. Her nipples hardened and molten heat pooled between her legs. Desire whipped through her and she had to fight not to tremble.

A one-night stand. That was what he was suggesting, wasn't it? How disgraceful. How offensive. And, what with the lust hurtling around inside her, how completely and deliciously tempting.

'That's outrageous,' she breathed, sounding less than convincing.

'Is it?'

'I might be concussed.'

'Are you?'

'Well, no, I don't think so, but that's not the point.'

'Then what is?'

'We barely know each other.'

'So?'

'I don't do that sort of thing.'

'Neither do I.'

'Then why me? Why now?'

A muscle ticked in his jaw and his eyes burned with desire. 'Because of this,' he muttered fiercely, closing the short distance between them, wrapping her in his arms and slamming his mouth down on hers.

Laura didn't have time to protest. Didn't have time to resist. Because the minute his lips touched hers what little rational thought she had left shattered. Fire licked through her veins. Beneath his mouth she moaned. Wound her arms round his neck and threaded her fingers through his hair. Pressed herself closer, parted her lips and felt her entire body soften.

When his tongue slipped into her mouth, seeking hers, finding hers, her knees buckled. If she hadn't been locked in his arms she'd have crumpled to the floor.

Sensation after sensation cascaded over her. Matt slid his hand over her waist, stroked it up her side and cupped her breast. Laura shuddered as his thumb brushed over her straining nipple and arched her back.

Drowning in pleasure, she sank into his kiss. No one had ever done this to her before, she thought dazedly. No one had ever turned her bones to water with nothing more than a kiss and a caress.

And she wasn't sure she'd ever done this to anyone, either. Matt was kissing her as if it were his sole mission in life. So focused. So damn good. His mouth seemed to have been made for hers. She fitted his hands perfectly. He would fit her perfectly.

A wave of lust rolled over her and she couldn't stop herself tilting her hips and rubbing herself against the rock-hard length of him.

Her control began to spin away and, totally unsure of whether to be scared witless or tumble him down onto the sofa, she gave in to the pleasure.

When Matt finally lifted his head, she could hardly breathe. Unlocking his arms from around her, he took a step back, his eyes blazing and his breathing jerky.

At the sudden absence of his support, his heat, Laura shivered and swayed for a second.

'That's why,' he said, drawing in a ragged breath and shoving his hands through his hair.

Laura blinked and touched her lips with trembling fingers. 'That's why what?'

'Why you.' His eyes, still dark and unfathomable, gleamed. 'As for the why now, well, I have the entire weekend free.'

Ah. 'I see,' she said a little shakily.

'You know,' he said, looking at her as if he wanted to devour her all over again, 'I really think you should cancel those plans of yours.'

Burning up beneath the heat of his gaze, Laura suddenly couldn't remember why she'd mentioned the non-existent plans in the first place.

Her heart skipped a beat. Oh, heavens. She wasn't seriously contemplating what he was suggesting, was she? She'd be mad to agree. She barely knew him. It was insane. She didn't do one-night stands. Had never wanted to. She preferred to date, assess and evaluate before leaping into bed with someone.

But where had that sensible, cautious approach ever got her? Dumped, that was where. Relationships sucked. Relationships belonged to the old Laura. Why shouldn't one-night stands belong to the new?

Besides, to have someone want her with this intensity, this hunger, when she'd been so recently rejected by someone she'd been with for years…

Her self-esteem, which had taken such a battering, was already rocketing. And to want someone quite this badly, when she'd thought she'd never be interested in anyone ever again, was heady stuff.

Her breath caught.

Standing in front of her was the most devastatingly gorgeous man she'd ever met. Who for some reason appeared to fancy her rotten. Would it really be so bad to go for it?

Suddenly sick and tired of evaluation and analysis, Laura made up her mind. 'How long are you here for?'

'I'm leaving tomorrow.'

'Are you planning to come back any time soon?'

'No.' His eyes bore into hers, burning with desire but offering nothing, apart from an afternoon of unimaginable pleasure.

Laura's heart pounded. That did it. No mess. No threat of entanglement in another debilitating relationship. Just the promise of hot sex and maybe lunch. 'OK, then.'

For a big man he moved surprisingly fast.

Even though she was ready for it, had been waiting for it, sort of knew what to expect, nothing could have prepared her for the sheer force of the desire that slammed through her at the feel of his arms whipping round her and the touch of his mouth to hers. The floor beneath her feet rocked. Her entire body buzzed with sensation.

Now that she made the decision to go for it, it was as if a dam had burst deep inside her. Any inhibitions she might have had fled.

His hands settled on the bare skin of her back and the electricity that flowed through her made her nerve endings jump.

She pressed herself closer, rubbing her aching breasts against his chest, needing the friction to provide some sort of relief.

As he explored her mouth with his tongue, Laura

slipped her hands beneath his T-shirt and ran them over the muscles of his back, pushing the fabric up. She felt him tense and break off the kiss for a second while he pulled the T-shirt over his head and tossed it onto the floor. Then his hands were at the hem of her top and seconds later it joined his.

Somewhere deep in the recesses of her mind she thought she ought to be faintly embarrassed at getting naked with someone she didn't know. Or at her desperation to have him inside her at the very least. But with his mouth sliding over her jaw, her neck and then down over the slope of her breast, Laura couldn't feel anything except the mindless pleasure sweeping over her.

Cupping his hands under her bottom, Matt lifted her and she wound her legs round his waist as he carried her to the nearest available flat surface. He set her on the edge of a table and began to push her back.

Laura's blood roared in her ears as she eased back but then she caught something out of the corner of her eye and went still. 'Wait.'

Matt jerked back and frowned down at her. 'What?'

'We can't do this.'

The blood drained from his face and his features turned grim. 'Are you serious?'

'Deadly.' She paused and caught her lip. 'At least we can't do this *here*.'

'Why not?'

Laura glanced down at what she was perched on and then back up at him. Poor Matt looked as if he were about to explode with frustration. 'This is a solid mahogany Regency breakfast table. It must be worth thousands.'

Matt let out a sharp breath and his expression relaxed. 'Then it was built to last,' he said, planting his hands either side of her and setting his mouth to the side of her neck.

'It was built to have breakfast on,' Laura said, putting a hand on his chest and nudging him away. 'Not wild uncontrollable sex.'

He lifted his head and one corner of his mouth hitched. 'Wild uncontrollable sex, huh?'

'You promised.'

'Did I?'

Laura nodded. 'Not in so many words. But these kisses of yours suggest a lot. I'm expecting combustion at the very least. And if we stay here I won't be able to concentrate.'

'Well, we can't have that,' he murmured. 'I doubt the insurance would cover sex-induced fire damage.' Pulling her upright, he glanced around. 'Do you have any such concerns about the sofa?'

Laura wound her arms around his neck. 'Is it flame-proof?'

'I should imagine so.'

'In that case,' she said, smiling up at him, 'none at all.'

'I can't tell you how glad I am to hear it.' He scooped her up and strode over to the sofa.

Setting her on her feet, he unclipped her bra and let it drop to the floor. 'These hot pants are going to haunt my dreams,' he said roughly, dragging them together with her knickers down her legs.

'You want me to apologise?' she breathed as she kicked them away.

'I want you to want this as much as I do,' he said, stripping off the rest of his clothes and tumbling her onto the sofa.

'I do,' she said, drawing in a shuddery breath as she

ran her gaze over him. God, his body was every bit as incredible as she'd imagined. Muscled, powerful, lean and tanned.

And any minute now it was all going to come down on top of her. Her gaze dropped to his erection and for a second she went dizzy. 'Oh, I *really* do.' She bit her lip to stop herself whimpering. 'More probably.'

'I doubt that's possible,' Matt said tightly.

Laura let her gaze wander up him, over the dips and ridges of his chest, the strong tanned neck and the square jaw and into eyes so dark they were almost black.

She swallowed and delicious anticipation began to thunder through her. Matt was radiating so much tension, looking as if he was having to battle so hard to cling on to his control that she wondered with a thrill what would happen when it snapped.

God, she thought with a tiny surge of satisfaction. Going for what she wanted was great. The sense of power it gave her was awesome. Who knew?

Lifting her arms above her head, Laura arched her back and batted her eyelashes as she smiled up at him. 'Why don't you come down here and join me and we can figure it out?'

'Just so you know,' he murmured, lowering himself on top of her and bearing his weight on his elbows, 'I always win.'

'I'm sure you do,' she said softly, loving the feel of his body trapping hers. Look where she was. But that didn't mean she couldn't at least try. 'You know what I'd really like?'

'What?'

She lifted her face and looked straight into his eyes. 'I'd like you inside me. Right now.'

She felt his heart thump. Saw his jaw clench. Felt his

whole body tighten. Aha. Who was winning now? 'Is that right?' he murmured, staring down at her but not moving an inch.

'It is,' she said softly.

'I'll bear it in mind.'

Oh. That wasn't the outcome she'd hoped for. 'Please…' she breathed, batting her eyelashes and smiling up at him.

His erection leapt. Feeling a tiny stab of triumph, she tilted her hips against him and let out a sigh of longing.

Matt growled. 'You,' he said, his mouth tugging into a faint smile, 'are irresistible.'

'I know,' she said smugly, and then gasped as his mouth landed on hers.

Hot and demanding, it began a devastating assault on her senses. His tongue drove into her mouth, tangling with hers, pushing her to the edge of reason. His hands settled on her arms above her head and then slid down her body, making her burn and tremble.

He dragged his mouth away from hers and dropped a trail of scorching kisses along her jaw and down her neck. Her head fell back and she moaned. His mouth moved lower, lower, until it closed over her aching nipple and she nearly leapt off the sofa. But he was pinning her down with his weight and all she could do was succumb.

Frankly why would she want to do anything else? Laura clutched a cushion with one hand. Grabbed his head with the other as he sucked, stroked, licked and nibbled and she started to lose it. Great waves of pleasure began to roll over her. Desire drenched her and she ached with the need to be filled with him.

'Please, Matt,' she breathed, no longer conscious of what she was saying. 'I don't think I can bear it.'

His mouth still on her breast, Matt swept his hand down over her hip, round, covered the triangle of hair at the top of her thighs and slid a finger deep inside her. Laura groaned and felt her inner muscles tighten around his finger. He pressed her clitoris with his thumb and her breathing shallowed as she felt herself begin to break apart.

No, she cried silently, clinging on to her control, she didn't want it to be like this.

She wanted him, all of him, all that strength pounding into her.

She wanted him to lose control the way she was about to.

'Are you going to make me beg again?'

'Would you?'

'If I have to. But I'd probably hate you for it.'

Matt let out a ragged breath. 'I wouldn't want that,' he murmured.

'Then help me out here,' she said desperately, dimly aware that he was leaning down and fumbling around on the floor. The sound of a packet tearing, the rolling on of a condom barely registered.

Every inch of her was aching, desperate with need. Biting her lip, she felt him pushing her knees apart, felt him nudging at her entrance and then thrusting forward, up, deep.

Laura gasped. Matt stopped. Waited a second for her to adjust. And then he pulled out of her, caught her mouth with his and drove back into her. A sob of pure pleasure rising in her throat, Laura wrapped her legs around his waist, threw her arms around his back and kissed him with every drop of desire she was feeling.

Her nails raked over his skin. His muscles strained with the effort of restraint.

But she didn't want restraint. She burned for release. Tearing her mouth from his, she breathed, 'More,' into his ear and lifted her hips.

Matt went utterly still. His eyes blazed and then he began to move. Harder, faster, deeper, driving her higher and higher, making something inside her coil tighter and tighter until he thrust one more time and sent her hurtling over the edge. Laura shattered into kaleidoscopic ecstasy. Wave after wave of pleasure poured over her as she convulsed and trembled. Her heart hammered. Her blood roared in her ears. She felt Matt's whole body tense. Heard him groan and then felt him pulsate deep inside her and it was enough to set off a series of tiny aftershocks of ecstasy that took her breath away all over again.

It was quite a few minutes before she got her breath and her senses back. As she drifted back down to reality after the most exquisite orgasm of her life she felt a great grin spreading across her face. Wow. If she'd known all casual sex was as hot as this, she'd have tried it long ago.

Or at least been a damn sight more assertive in the bedroom.

One softly breathed word and Matt's steely control had unravelled. Still cocooned in the warmth of his arms, Laura felt like purring with pleasure. She'd have to remember that in the future.

And then she froze. Her heart thumped. Uh-oh. The future? That didn't sound good. That sounded as if she wanted a repeat. Lots of repeats in fact. Repeats that went way beyond one afternoon.

To her horror she could feel her body softening, heating, getting ready for more just as soon as possible.

'Laura?' Matt's voice cut through the hazy fog in her head.

'Hmm?' She wasn't entirely sure she could speak and not just because his chest was crushing her lungs.

He lifted his head and looked down at her, his eyes unfathomable. 'Are you all right?'

'Fine,' she muttered, thinking she was anything but.

God, she was such an idiot. Had she really thought she could get rid of her old self that easily? That one two-week course, albeit a highly intensive one, could undo the habits of thirty-one years? What a pillock.

If she didn't get out of here this very moment she'd find herself being sucked in by Matt and the incredible orgasms he appeared to be able to give her and she'd end up wanting more. Which was most certainly not part of the deal she'd made with either herself or him.

Laura swallowed and fixed a smile to her face. 'Couldn't be better,' she added lightly.

Matt frowned. 'Are you sure?'

Agh. This was so not a conversation she wanted to be having with him still hard and deep inside her. 'Absolutely.' She nodded, gave him a quick smile and prodded at his shoulders. 'Would you mind?'

'I rather think I would,' Matt said flatly, manoeuvring them to shift himself onto his back and pulling her on top of him.

The blast of cold air that hit her back made Laura shiver. 'Could you let me go, please?'

His arms fell from her waist, and she eased herself off him. Aware that his eyes were following her every move, burning into her skin, Laura fought the impulse to leap back on top of him, and set about retrieving her clothes. She swiped up her underwear and her T-shirt and dragged them on, trying not to respond to the way they scratched over her already highly sensitised skin.

Her shorts, however, lay beneath him. Laura bit her lip. Sprinting back home without them would encourage curtain twitching gossip she definitely didn't need. 'Can you shift a bit?' she said, trying to yank on the inch of fabric she could see.

However Matt didn't budge. Apart from shooting his hand out to wrap itself round her wrist.

'Laura, what's going on?'

'Going on?' she said, her eyes jerking to his. Only minutes ago his eyes had been blazing with passion but his whole demeanour was stonier than granite. 'Nothing's going on.'

'So why the hurry?'

'I have to get going.'

'A little too wild and uncontrollable, huh?'

She stamped down on the blush that she could feel blooming inside her. 'Not at all,' she said, aiming for a nonchalance she didn't feel. 'I really do have to go. Like I said, I have plans.'

Matt released her, sprang to his feet and yanked on his jeans. 'Right,' he said, his voice ice cold and devoid of emotion. 'Sure. Then I guess you don't want lunch.'

With him standing there looking so gorgeous and rumpled in just his jeans, all Laura could think of was how much she did want lunch. With Matt as the main course. 'Some other time perhaps,' she muttered, and legged it.

CHAPTER FIVE

THREE weeks later, Laura had just about managed to wipe Matt and that incredible afternoon from her mind. But it had been one of the hardest things she'd ever had to do.

For days afterwards she'd wafted around in a kind of dreamlike state, not entirely sure whether the whole thing had actually happened or if it had simply been a product of her imagination. It had been so amazing, so mind-blowing and, up until the moment she'd panicked, everything she'd imagined it would be.

Ruthlessly blocking out the way they'd parted, or rather the way she'd scarpered, she'd wallowed in the memories of the hour before, and as a result had got very little done.

If it hadn't been for the call from the headhunter a week ago she'd probably still be at it. Wandering round her house with a dreamy smile on her face, putting the milk in the bathroom cabinet and the toothpaste in the fridge.

To think that she might have missed out on the opportunity of a lifetime just because she'd been too busy drifting around in a daze…

Laura went cold and shuddered. It didn't bear thinking about. And neither did Matt. Not any longer. Now she had to focus on her career. Her savings wouldn't last for ever and daydreaming wouldn't pay the bills.

This job, however, would not only pay the bills, it would also get her life firmly back on track.

The opportunity to head up the restoration project on the isolated island of Sassania was a dream come true. The country had been closed off to the outside world for years. As the result of a recent coup, the dictatorship had been overthrown and the borders had been thrown wide open.

The island had some of the finest examples of Baroque architecture in the world. Palaces and monuments she'd only ever read about. Palaces and monuments that were currently in a terrible state of repair and needed restoring.

Ideally, by her.

She'd emailed her CV to the headhunter virtually the moment she'd put the phone down, and to her delight had received a reply the next day inviting her for an interview.

Which was why she was now in London, taking her best friend out for dinner in return for a bed for the night before catching her crack-of-dawn flight in the morning.

'So how is life in the country?' said Kate, plucking the umbrella out of her cocktail and taking a long slurp.

Dragging herself away from dusty palaces in tiny Mediterranean island kingdoms and back to trendy London restaurants, Laura picked up a fat juicy olive from the bowl and glanced across the table. 'Quiet.'

'I can imagine.'

No, she couldn't, but there was no way Laura was going to elaborate on what she'd been up to. Not when she'd just managed to stop thinking about it. 'How's the world of corporate law?'

Kate took another sip of her cocktail and sighed with pleasure. 'Yum yum. You know, the usual. Nutty hours, problems galore and clients with egos the size of planets. I don't know why I do it.'

'Because you love it.'

Kate grinned. 'I guess I do.' She tilted her head. 'Don't you miss all this?'

Laura glanced around the place Kate had suggested for dinner. A brand-new London restaurant that had shot to the top of the uber-cool lists the day after it had opened.

Against the deep red silk lining of the walls hung enormous canvases by some on-the-up artist. Tiny chandeliers hung above every one of the slate-grey tables, casting flatteringly low sparkling light over the clientele. Model-like waiters who were far too sultry and hip to ever crack a smile whizzed around with plates of food that looked beautiful and made her mouth water. The chatter was low, buzzing and probably far more sophisticated than she was.

Not all that long ago Laura had spent many of her evenings and weekends in places like this. Now she felt a bit like a foreigner.

'Not really,' she muttered, slightly perturbed by the realisation.

'I don't know how you can bear it,' said Kate with a tiny shudder. 'I mean, no shops, no bars and all that greenery.' She wrinkled her nose. 'It's just not natural.'

Stifling a smile at the irony, Laura shrugged. 'I muddle along.'

'But that's my point,' Kate said. 'You don't have to

muddle along. I mean, I know things went a bit pear-shaped, but why you had to run off to the country is beyond me.'

A bit pear-shaped? 'Yes, well, when your life implodes as spectacularly as mine did you can end up doing all sorts of out-of-character things.'

'You could have come and stayed with me.'

Kate sounded a little piqued, and Laura gave her a smile. 'I know. And I did appreciate the offer, but it was something I needed to sort out on my own.'

Plus Kate would have given her heaps of advice, which she'd have insisted Laura follow, and Laura would have been too wiped out to argue.

But not any more. No more taking the easy way out. No more falling in with other people's wishes all the time. If her afternoon with Matt had taught her one thing it was that going for what *she* wanted for a change could achieve some pretty spectacular results.

Not that she was thinking about him of course, she reminded herself, picking up a menu and letting her gaze drift over the other diners. The restaurant was packed with some seriously beautiful people. Not a hint of last year's fashion, nor an un-touched-up root in sight. She was surprised they'd let her in.

And to be honest she was kind of dreading the bill. Laura resisted the urge to slap herself on the forehead with her menu. She'd done it again, hadn't she? Gulped back a knot of panic when Kate had suggested this place, and said, yes, sure, why not.

Why, oh, why hadn't she been firmer, and told Kate they'd be going to the little Italian around the corner from her flat?

Feeling her spirits tumble, Laura's gaze bobbed across the room. She bet none of the people here was quite so feeble. No. They'd all be decisive and in charge. They wouldn't flounder around and let others ride roughshod all over them.

And then her eyes snagged on a broad back and dark head and her heart practically stopped.

Oh, Lord. That looked just like Matt.

For a second Laura went dizzy. Then her heart began to gallop and heat whipped through every inch of her body. What was he doing here? Would he see her? Would he come over? What would she say if he did? What would she do if he *didn't*?

Her chest squeezed. Her mouth went dry. Oh, God. If he did come over she wouldn't just have to deal with him. She'd also have to deal with Kate, whose razor-sharp instinct would instantly pick up on the atmosphere, and who'd wring out every tiny detail and then hammer Laura with a barrage of 'what were you thinking?'s and 'but it's so unlike you's.

Laura took a deep breath and forced herself to calm down before her head exploded. It would be fine. She was a mature sensible adult who'd been through far worse. She'd simply channel the inner Amazon she was sure was lurking somewhere inside her, and be strong.

Nevertheless when all six foot plus of him got to his feet she caught and held her breath. Her pulse thundered. The blood rushed to her feet. He turned. Gave her a glimpse of his face.

And disappointment walloped her in the stomach.

It wasn't Matt.

Letting her breath out before she fainted, Laura blinked and turned her attention back to the menu. Of course it wouldn't have been Matt, she told herself sternly. That would have been too much of a coincidence and she didn't believe in coincidences.

She frowned and scanned the dishes. The weird sensation whirling around inside her wasn't disappointment. It was relief. That was all.

'Quiet?' said Kate. 'Hah! I knew it. So who is he?'

Laura froze and glanced up. The gleam in her friend's eye looked far too knowing for her liking. 'Who is who?' she said deliberately vaguely.

'The man that's put the weird look on your face.'

Laura's heart lurched. 'That's not a man,' she muttered. 'That's the dim lighting.' She squinted at the menu. 'In fact I can barely read this. Maybe I need glasses.' She held it up to the beautiful but fairly useless light that hung above the table.

'Rubbish,' said Kate.

'I definitely need a dictionary.'

'You look as if you've just had the fright of your life.'

'Well, I haven't.' Except perhaps at the prices. 'Whatever you're thinking you're wrong.'

'No, I'm not. I'm a lawyer. I'm known for my tenacity and trained to notice things.'

But not, apparently, the waiter who, with exquisite timing, was hovering at their table ready to take their order.

Laura looked up at him and gave her saviour a wide smile. 'I was wondering…what is the *rouget*?'

'Red mullet, madam.'

'Thank you. And the *poêlée de châtaignes*?'

'Pan-fried chestnuts.'

There were two pages of dishes. With any luck by the time she'd got to the bottom of the second page, Kate might have got bored and moved on.

Hmm. Or perhaps not, she thought as Kate swiped

the menu out of her hands and beamed up at the waiter. 'I'll have the lamb and she'll have the sea bass.'

Huh. Laura waited until he'd melted away before scowling at her friend.

'What?' said Kate, arching an eyebrow.

'I'm perfectly capable of ordering for myself.'

'I know, but I have a feeling there's a story to be told and we don't have all night. Besides you always have sea bass'

Laura stiffened. 'Maybe I was thinking about trying something different.'

Kate gave a little snort of disbelief. 'You were stalling. And when have you ever tried something different?'

Laura bristled. Was she really so boringly predictable? 'That's not fair. I do try different things.'

'Like what?' Kate's eyes zoomed in on her.

Like jumping into bed with scorchingly hot neighbours. Not that she intended to use *that* as an example. 'Fine.' She shrugged as if she couldn't be less bothered, and took a sip of her drink. 'I don't. Boring and predictable, that's me.'

Kate's blue gaze turned piercing. 'I think you lie.'

'Think what you like.'

'Come on,' said Kate, adding a wheedling smile to the penetrating stare. 'I know something's up and it's got "man" written all over it. I'm not going to give up until you tell me so you might as well give in now and get it over with.'

Not for the first time, Laura could see why Kate was so successful at what she did. Dogs and bones sprang to mind. Stifling a sigh, she weighed up her options. Denial and a battle with Kate's formidable persistence, which would last all evening, or half an hour of interrogation, which would be sharp but probably short and would allow her to enjoy the rest of her sea bass.

Hmm. If she wanted to be on top form for tomorrow she didn't have much of a choice. 'OK,' she said, bracing herself, 'you're right.'

'Aha.' Kate grinned in triumph. 'I knew it.' She signalled for two more drinks and sat back. 'You'd better tell me everything.'

Ten minutes and two cocktails later, Laura had finished her rundown of almost everything, and was now watching her friend with faint amusement. She didn't think she'd ever seen Kate lost for words before. She was sitting there, her eyes wide and her jaw almost on the floor. Even the arrival of their food didn't snap Kate out of her state of shock.

Laura decided to leave her to it and tucked in. Popping a forkful of fish in her mouth, she sighed in appreciation. As annoyingly hip as the restaurant was, the food was spectacular.

'Well,' said Kate, eventually pulling herself together and regaining the ability to speak.

'Your lamb is getting cold,' Laura pointed out.

'Sod the lamb,' Kate said, still looking on utterly shell-shocked. 'Let me get this straight. You ogle. You engage in confrontation. You stand your ground. And then you have sex with a man you've only just met.'

'Yes.' Laura took another mouthful and decided that for all the benefits of the countryside, it didn't do food like this.

Kate's mouth opened then closed. 'To be honest I don't know which part of the whole thing I'm more shocked by.'

'I thought it was time for a change.' Hah. Who was predictable now?

'Have you seen him since?'

'No.' She'd known he'd stayed the rest of the weekend but he'd kept himself to himself. Not that she'd been keeping a special eye out or anything.

'Do you intend to?'

'Absolutely not. It was a one-night—afternoon—stand. Non-repetition is kind of the point.'

There was another long silence as Kate absorbed this information. 'Who are you and what have you done with my friend?'

'Ha-ha.'

'I knew moving to the country was dangerous,' Kate muttered, picking up her knife and fork and attacking her lamb. 'You're unhinged.'

Undoubtedly. But that had happened long before she'd met Matt. 'If I am,' said Laura darkly as the image of her ex-boyfriend in bed with his secretary flashed into her head, 'it has nothing to do with geography.'

Kate gave her a sympathetic smile. 'No, well, I suppose I can see why you might need a bit of an ego boost. Lying cheating bastard.'

Laura couldn't help smiling at the disgust in Kate's voice. 'Yup.'

'You know, I still can't believe he did that. To you of all people.' Kate shook her head in bafflement. 'I mean, you're one of the most easy-going people I know.'

'Too easy-going apparently.'

'What?'

'Paul said that I was partly to blame for his affair.'

Kate's jaw dropped. 'The cheek,' she muttered. 'How did he work that one out?'

'He said I was too acquiescent. That if I'd stood up to him a bit more, been a bit more demanding, he might have thought twice about bonking his secretary.'

'The complete and utter snake.'

Laura caught her lip between her teeth and frowned. 'But maybe he did have a point. He kept calling me babe, and not once did I tell him not to even though I hated it.'

'It used to make me wince.'

'Me, too.' Laura grimaced. 'Anyway I've had time to think about it and, you know, I *have* been a bit of a pushover.'

'Rubbish.'

'So why do I end up giving the old people in the village lifts left, right and centre?'

'Because you're a nice person.'

'Huh.' Laura frowned. 'I have a backbone of rubber. Well, not any more.'

'So what's the plan?'

'I've already put it into action.'

'So I can see.'

'Not that,' she said, batting back a blush. 'The minute I moved to the country I enrolled on an assertiveness course.'

Kate's eyebrows shot up. 'Wow.'

'I know.' Laura nodded. 'We learned to Embrace Confrontation, Say No With Confidence and to Go For What *You* Want.'

'So you embraced confrontation and went for the afternoon of hot sex that you wanted.'

'Quite.' Something kicked in the pit of her stomach.

Kate grinned. 'I can't imagine there was a whole lot of saying no, either with confidence or without it.'

'Not a lot.' Just rather a lot of breathy yeses.

'Well, I'm not sure about the rest of it, but that's one way to get a lousy ex out of your system.'

'That's what I thought.'

Kate tilted her head and looked at Laura with something resembling admiration. 'Reckless. Totally out of character. I like it.'

Laura felt a shiver run down her spine. 'So did I.' She nibbled on her lip and frowned. Up until the point she'd panicked and fled. That had been cowardly.

'I'm so envious.' Kate sighed. 'Remind me why you aren't going to see him again.'

Laura shrugged. 'It wasn't like that. The temporariness of it was what was so appealing.' Well, one of the things. 'We didn't exchange numbers.'

'I'm sure he'd be in the phone book. Have you Googled him?'

'Of course not.' She hadn't given in to the temptation yet and she didn't intend to.

'Why not?'

'I don't want to see him again.'

'That's nuts. Great sex isn't something to be dismissed lightly.'

'It hasn't changed anything,' said Laura firmly, before she started agreeing with Kate and waving goodbye to all her good intentions. 'I'm still off men. And I need another relationship like I need a hole in the head.'

'But you're always in a relationship.' Kate frowned.

'Exactly. And look what happens. I get smothered. I lose sense of my own identity and allow myself to get walked all over. And ultimately get hurt.' She shrugged. 'I've had enough.'

'Well, I think you're mad.' Kate sniffed.

Laura smiled. 'Actually I've never felt saner in my life. Which is just as well if I'm going to get this job. Now, let's have pudding.'

CHAPTER SIX

HE'D been right about those damn hot pants, thought Matt grimly, glancing at his watch and noting he had five minutes before his meeting with the finance minister to discuss exactly how deep the corruption that had burrowed into pretty much every governmental department went.

They *did* haunt his dreams. As, to his intense irritation, did Laura.

It was bad enough that the minute he crashed into bed there she was, her hair fanning out over his cushions, her eyes shimmering and glazed with desire as she stared up at him and saying 'more' and 'please' in that breathy desperate way she had.

It was bad enough that he woke up pretty much every morning, aching and throbbing and twitching with desire.

But what was really driving him nuts was the lack of control he seemed to have over his thoughts while he was awake.

She kept popping up, shooting smouldering smiles at him, and the memory of the way she'd exploded and shuddered in his arms would slam into his head and his train of thought would derail and his body would react with annoying inevitability.

Like now.

Feeling uncomfortably hot and growing painfully hard, Matt scowled, got up and stalked over to the window.

Quite why Laura should be taking up so much of his head space when she'd been just a one-night stand and when he had plenty of other things to occupy his mind was baffling.

OK, so the way she'd run off like that had hardly been flattering but it wasn't as if he'd intended on seeing her again, was it? She clearly had issues and that wasn't his problem. And yes, the sex had been incredible, but it had been three weeks ago. He really ought to have got over it by now.

Matt threw open the window and inhaled deeply. He'd have liked a nice icy blast of around minus five to relieve the hot achiness of his body. But unfortunately Sassania was in the Mediterranean not the Baltic, and this being early summer all that drifted in through the window was a soft balmy breeze.

Stifling a groan of frustration, he yanked open the top buttons of his shirt and made a mental note to get someone to investigate the air-conditioning options. Then at least he'd be able to control the temperature, if nothing else.

He was just about to turn back to grab his laptop and head off to his meeting when he heard the rap of heels on stone and caught a movement out of the corner of his eye.

Something, he had no idea what, made him pause. Made him train his focus on the woman walking across the patio.

For some reason his breathing faltered. The floor beneath his feet lurched. His pulse jumped. She was walking away from him, and he couldn't be sure, but that looked just like Laura.

Matt blinked and gave his head a quick shake. No. That was nuts. It couldn't be Laura. Because what would she be doing in *his* palace on *his* island? It was his feverish imagination working overtime, that was all. Lack of sleep, too, probably. And this damn stifling heat.

Nevertheless something about the way she moved had his eyes narrowing and awareness prickling his skin. Maybe it was the graceful sway of her hips. Or maybe it was the way she suddenly reached up to tuck a lock of hair behind her ear. She might be wearing a nifty little suit instead of a T-shirt and hot pants, but those curves looked very familiar.

As she stopped and turned to say something to the security guard accompanying her Matt caught a glimpse of her face and any lingering doubt fled.

His head swam for a second. His heart pounded. Hell. It *was* Laura.

He ran a hand over his face. Rubbed his eye and pinched the bridge of his nose. Then frowned.

What on earth was she doing here?

Had she come to apologise?

Had she decided she wanted more than just a one-night stand?

Or had she come to see what she could get out of their brief liaison?

She wouldn't be the first, Matt thought, his mouth twisting into a cynical smile as he shoved his hands in his pockets and watched her gazing at the pillars and arches of the colonnades that surrounded the patio.

Several of the women he'd known in the past had got in touch to suggest that if he was ever on the lookout for a queen they'd be more than happy to occupy the position. And more than willing to provide heirs.

If Matt could have been bothered to reply he'd have told them they were wasting their time. Marriage and children did not feature on his agenda. He'd been engaged once and look what a disaster that had been. No. His jaw tightened. He wasn't even cut out for a relationship, let alone anything more, so anyone who hoped otherwise could think again.

But if any of his suspicions were correct about Laura's presence on Sassania, why hadn't she asked to be led straight to him? Why was she now shaking the hand of his culture minister?

Matt frowned as his mind raced. Then the brief conversation he'd had with Giuseppe Ragazzi about the state of the country's public buildings and the urgent need to restore them flashed into his head and realisation dawned.

Oh, damn. His heart sank. Laura was here for the job.

With the arrest of the former president on his mind at the time, he'd agreed to the request to hire an architect without really thinking about it. Now, he thought, his jaw tightening, he ought to have paid more attention. Imposed certain conditions, at the very least. Such as not engaging the services of one Laura Mackenzie.

No way could she be given the job. If she got the job she'd be there. In the palace. All the time. Screwing up his concentration and messing with his head. What with everything else going on, he did *not* need that kind of complication.

Laura held her breath. She'd done everything she could. She'd answered all the questions she'd been asked confidently and correctly. Outlined the vision she had for Sassania's public buildings. Talked passionately about the career she loved, and clarified the reasons for her redundancy.

Now she was waiting on tenterhooks while Signore Ragazzi flicked through her portfolio with agonising thoroughness.

She wanted this job so badly. Apart from the fact that the idea of working on something she'd drooled over at college made her chest squeeze with excitement, it was such a prestigious project.

If she got it, she'd be made. Her battered professional pride would recover and she'd have her pick of jobs. Her former employers would read the sensational series of articles she'd write for *Architecture Tomorrow* and shake their heads at their stupidity in getting rid of her quite so speedily.

But if she didn't… Where would that leave her?

The worries she'd managed to keep at bay crept into her head. What if Signore Ragazzi didn't like her work? What if they'd had thousands of other applicants, all of whom had more and better experience than she did? What if she wasn't up to the job? What if—?

Oh, for goodness' sake. Releasing her breath before she passed out, Laura gave herself a quick shake and pulled herself together. What was the point of working herself up into a state? She'd take whatever decision he came to graciously and professionally, and face the consequences later.

Nevertheless when Signore Ragazzi closed her portfolio and looked up, she had to sit on her hands to stop them from whipping up and covering her eyes. Which was a good thing because if she'd had her eyes covered she wouldn't have been able to see the wide smile he gave her.

Hope flared in her heart and her ears buzzed. Surely he wouldn't be smiling like that if he was going to say thanks but no thanks.

'Signorina Mackenzie,' he said, and her breath caught. 'I'm delighted to inform you that you have the job.'

The words took a couple of seconds to register. But when they did Laura felt like punching the air. Would it be completely inappropriate if she hurdled the desk, leapt into his lap and gave him a big kiss? Hmm. Perhaps. Just a little. Instead she settled for a grin. 'I do?'

He smiled and nodded. 'You do.'

A bubble of delight began to bounce round inside her. 'That's fantastic,' she said, thinking that was quite an understatement.

He opened a drawer and extracted a sheaf of papers. 'We think so. To be honest, you're the only person we've called in for an interview, so the outcome has never been in doubt. The only obstacle we had foreseen would have been your lack of availability.'

He pushed the document across the desk and Laura glanced down at it, faintly stunned. 'Oh.'

'I've seen your work before. The Church of St Mary the Virgin?' She managed a nod. 'I particularly liked your sense of balance.'

Crikey. She'd never felt less balanced. 'I'm so glad,' she murmured.

'We'd like to begin with the palace.'

'Of course.' Excitement clutched at her stomach. She'd studied every fabulous inch of the palace. Pored over photos and reports. Salivated over the flying buttresses and crumbling gargoyles and idolised every one of the six thousand windows. No amount of books and papers could get across the smell of the place, the vitality of the stone and the feel of the warm breeze on her skin when she'd stood outside the gate, the same warm breeze that must have caressed these walls for centuries. Walls that were now crumbling and collapsing.

'When would you be able to begin?'

Right now would be fine with her. Or would that seem a little desperate? Not to mention totally impractical. She'd come with only her passport and her toothbrush. She was going to need a lot more than that. 'In a week?'

'Excellent.' He beamed at her. 'I'll arrange for a suite to be made up for you.'

'Thank you.'

'If you'll just sign here…'

He handed her a pen and Laura felt thrills scurrying through her. She'd done it. She'd actually done it.

Well, of course she had, she told herself as she floated back down to reality and worked her way through the contract. Her personal life might be a bit of a disaster, but she'd always been good at her job.

'Will you excuse me?' said Signore Ragazzi, cutting across her musings and picking up the phone, which had just started to ring.

He could strip and dance round his desk naked if he felt like it, Laura thought, finally getting to the last page and signing on the dotted line. She was busy wondering where would be the best place to start. The public rooms undoubtedly. Then the private areas. The gardens… Oh, the possibilities were endless and she lost herself in them.

It was only when she heard her own name that her ears pricked.

'Yes, sir. Signorina Mackenzie has just accepted the position.'

Laura's heart swelled with pride. She'd do the best job she could. Achieve the sort of result people would talk about for years, long after she left. After centuries of decline the palace deserved it. After all she'd been through, *she* deserved it.

'Oh.' At the tone of his voice for some reason her nerve endings tensed. 'I'm afraid I can't retract the offer, sir.' His voice dropped. 'She's just signed the contract.'

Laura snapped her head up and stared at him. Someone wanted him to retract the offer? No, that couldn't be possible.

Signore Ragazzi fell silent, went red and swivelled round in his chair so she couldn't see him. 'Nor can I rip it up,' he added, his voice now dropping so low she had to strain to listen.

Rip it up? Who the hell was that on the other end of the line, and why did they not want her to have the job? What had she done to cause such offence? Had there been some sort of mistake and the job already been given to someone else? Laura's chest squeezed at the thought that she might have had her dream snatched from her at the very last minute.

'No, sir… Yes, sir… I'll see to it immediately.'

Signore Ragazzi swivelled back and gave her a smile too bright to be genuine.

Laura clasped her hands together in her lap to stop them from flapping. 'Is there a problem?' she asked, bracing herself for the answer to be yes and for him to laugh and tell her it was all just one big joke.

'No, no,' he said, gathering up the contract she'd just

signed in an effort, she suspected, to avoid eye contact. 'Just one more tiny formality.'

'Oh.'

He smoothed his hair, pushed his chair back and got up and indicated that she should do the same. 'If you wouldn't mind coming with me…'

'Of course,' Laura murmured, her heart beginning to thud. What on earth was going on?

The feeling of trepidation as she followed Signore Ragazzi didn't abate. In fact it swelled to such proportions that she barely noticed the busts on pedestals lining the corridor. Or the old masters hanging on the walls. The only thing hammering at her brain was that something didn't feel right.

Signore Ragazzi stopped in front of a pair of huge gilded doors and knocked. Laura's heart banged with consternation.

'Come in.'

At the sound of the voice from deep within, all the hairs at the back of her neck leapt up and her stomach clenched.

Something *wasn't* right.

Because if it hadn't been utterly impossible, she'd have sworn that that was Matt's voice coming from the room.

But it couldn't be Matt because that would be crazy. What would he be doing here?

No, Laura told herself, pulling her shoulders back, going through the doors that Signore Ragazzi held open and entering the room. First she'd thought she'd seen him in that restaurant in London. Now she imagined he was here? Hah. This was precisely why she'd vowed to have nothing whatsoever to do with men. They messed up your head. She was far better off sticking to inanimate objects like the crumbling cornice and the chipped reliefs that adorned this room.

Wow, she thought, her alarm momentarily vanishing as she looked up at the ceiling. Faded and dilapidated it might be, but it was still a magnificent room. And, she noted, letting her gaze drop and scan the space, an empty one. She hadn't noticed Signore Ragazzi melt away. Perhaps she'd imagined that 'come in', too.

'Hello, Laura.'

The deep lazy voice behind her nearly made her jump a foot in the air. Her heart lurched. She swung round and at the sight of the man leaning against the bookcase, his gaze pinned to her, the breath shot from her lungs. Shock and disbelief slammed through her.

Oh, good Lord. It *was* Matt.

Bewilderment clamoured at her brain. Her head went fuzzy, her blood zoomed to her feet and her vision blurred. Laura flung her arm out and grabbed on to the nearest thing to stop herself swooning.

The nearest thing happened to be Matt. For a second she clutched at his arm. But the feel of his muscles brought the memory of that afternoon careering back and she went dizzy all over again.

Jerking back, Laura dragged in a breath and willed the room to right itself.

No need to panic. There was bound to be some rational explanation for Matt being here. At this particular moment she couldn't imagine what it could possibly be, but she'd figure it out somehow.

Just as soon as her heart rate slowed and her breathing returned to normal. Which would happen a lot quicker if he didn't look quite so gorgeous. Wearing a pale blue shirt with the sleeves pushed up to his elbows and light brown chinos, he looked rumpled, incredibly sexy and oddly at home. His face was more tanned than when she'd last seen him and the lines around his mouth and eyes a little sharper, but if anything they just made him even more attractive.

Heat pooled in the pit of her stomach and began to spread through her body. Extinguishing it with a determination she hadn't known she possessed, Laura ran her palms down her skirt and fixed a neutral smile to her face. 'Matt,' she said as coolly as she could, as if she weren't completely clueless as to how to proceed. 'How lovely to see you again.'

'Quite.' He didn't look like he agreed. 'How's the bump?'

Laura blinked and tried not to think about the circumstances that had brought about the bang to her head or the consequences. 'Fine. How was the rest of your weekend?'

'Pleasingly uneventful.'

Oh. So he clearly hadn't spent any time drifting around in a daze. 'What are you doing here?'

'I live here.'

Right. Laura's mouth opened and then closed. She couldn't begin to work out where to start. Was he here for a job, too? 'Village mansions a little on the small side?'

The ghost of a smile played at his lips and Laura had the uncomfortable feeling that he knew everything while she knew nothing.

'It comes with my job.'

'What do you do?'

'Usually?'

How many jobs did he have? 'Yes.'

'I buy ailing businesses, turn them around and sell them for a profit.'

That didn't make things any clearer. 'Is that why you're here?'

'In a way.'

Laura frowned. 'But you were the "sir" on the other end of the line.'

Matt nodded. 'I was. Would you like to sit down?'

'No, I'm fine.'

'I think you should sit. You look a little pale.'

Was it any wonder? Laura thought, sinking into a leather library chair before her legs gave way. Baffled didn't begin to describe the way she was feeling. 'How did you know I was here?'

'I saw you from the window.'

So that would account for the weird tingling that she'd experienced while she'd been walking across the patio. The twitchy feeling that had made her stop and ask the security guard about mosquitoes.

'I don't get it,' she said, her eyebrows drawing together a fraction. 'I've just been contracted to restore the palace. Why does it have anything to do with you?'

Matt moved round to sit on the edge of the huge partners' desk. 'It's my palace.'

Maybe the state had given it to him in payment or something. Laura blinked but it didn't make her brain hurt any less. 'I'd have thought it would belong to the king.'

'It does.'

His expression was unreadable, his eyes unfathomable. Which was a shame as she could really do with a little help here. Absolutely nothing was making any sense.

If the palace belonged to the king and it also belonged to him, then that would mean that Matt was the king. Her brain might be about to explode but she could work that much out. And if he was king what had he been doing in Little Somerford? What had he been doing smouldering at her, tearing off her clothing and taking her to heaven and back?

God, it was a good thing she was sitting down.

'Who exactly are you?' she said, not at all sure she wanted to have the horrible suspicions flying around her head confirmed.

'You know who I am.'

'I thought I did. I thought you were Matt Saxon.' She gave a little shrug as if it didn't bother her one way or the other. 'It looks like I was wrong. Silly me.'

'You weren't. I am Matt Saxon. I happen to also be King of Sassania.'

Ah. There it was. Proof that she hadn't been going mad. At least not within the past five minutes.

Laura gulped, completely unable to unravel the swirling mass of emotions rolling around inside her. Maybe it would be best to stick to facts. 'Since when?'

'Three weeks ago.'

'Before or after we…' she broke off and went red '…you know…?'

'The coronation took place the Monday after the weekend when we…er, met.'

He gave her a little mocking smile and her cheeks flamed even more.

And then out of the tangle of emotions, indignation suddenly broke free and fuelled through her. How dared he laugh at her? It was all very well for him, perched there being all high and mighty. She was the one who was totally wrong-footed and struggling to get her head round what was happening. She had every right to be confused. And to demand some answers. 'And you didn't think to mention it?'

His eyebrows shot up at her sharp tone. 'Why would I? We didn't exactly stop to engage in small talk.'

Damn. That was true.

Matt tilted his head and shot her a quizzical glance. 'Did you really not know who I was?'

Laura scowled at him. 'I really didn't.'

'No, well,' he said, lifting himself off the desk and moving to sit behind it, 'I doubt the coronation was covered in *Architecture Tomorrow*.' Like that was an excuse. 'However if you remember I did suggest lunch, and if you hadn't run off quite so speedily I might have mentioned it then.'

Laura's eyes narrowed. Oh, he was clever. Turning it around so it was her fault. 'I'd like to believe that, but somehow I don't.'

Matt gave her a quick grin that curled her toes. 'We'll never know now, will we?'

Unfortunately not. 'What were you doing in Little Somerford?'

'Escaping the press.'

No wonder he'd flipped when he'd thought she was a journalist. He was gorgeous, young, rich and royal. A paparazzo's dream. And she hadn't had a clue. She really ought to broaden her reading horizons.

'And you got me instead.'

'Briefly.' The grin faded and his mouth twisted.

Hmm. Laura bit back the urge to apologise. Any previous notion she might have had of apologising had long since disappeared beneath a blanket of confusion, indignation and something that felt suspiciously like hurt. 'You sound peeved,' she said coolly.

He raised an eyebrow. 'Well, the speed with which you fled wasn't particularly flattering.'

A smidgeon of guilt elbowed its way through her

indignation. Laura shrugged and ignored it. 'We had a quickie. It was no big deal.'

His eyes glittered. 'If it was no big deal why did you run?'

'Like I told you at the time, I had plans.'

'Right.'

He fixed her with a gaze that had her squirming in her chair until she couldn't stand it any longer. So much for thinking she might have had the upper hand. Matt made one formidable opponent.

'OK, fine,' she said, throwing her hands up in exasperation. 'I guess I panicked.'

'Why?'

'I'm not entirely sure,' she said, forcing herself to look him in the eye. 'It was kind of intense. For me, at least. I don't know. Maybe for you it's like that all the time.'

'Not all the time,' he muttered, looking less than thrilled by the admission.

At his obvious discomfort Laura suddenly relaxed. 'It was kind of amazing, wasn't it?'

'Hmm.'

Matt regarded her thoughtfully and she bit her lip. It wasn't his fault she'd been spooked. He didn't know about the battle she'd had with herself. And now it seemed that fate had decided they were going to have to work together. Unless she cleared the air the tension that simmered between them would soon reach an unbearable level. 'I'm sorry I rushed off like that.'

He shrugged. 'It really doesn't matter. I put it out of my mind weeks ago.'

'Oh,' she said, stamping down on the perverse disappointment that he could dismiss it quite so easily.

'Well, that's good, seeing as we're going to be working together.'

Matt's gaze jerked to hers and his eyebrows shot up. 'You don't really think you can stay, do you?'

Laura went very still and felt her face pale. 'What do you mean?'

He leaned forwards and clasped his hands on the desk. 'I appreciate the fact that you've been given the job, and I realise there's nothing I can do contractually, but in the light of our recent history don't you think it would be wise if you refused?'

What? Refuse? He wanted her to give up the job she so badly needed? Over her dead body. Sticking her chin up, she fixed him with a firm stare. 'No.'

For a second there was a stunned silence. Matt looked as if she'd slapped him. Clearly no one had ever said no to him before. Well, that was tough, thought Laura, folding her arms over her chest and crossing her legs. Her days of endless people pleasing, of always acquiescing, were over.

'No?'

'Absolutely not,' she added, setting her jaw and glaring at him just in case he still didn't get the message. 'I'm not going anywhere.'

Matt's brows snapped together and he shoved a hand through his hair. 'There's a conflict of interest,' he said tightly.

'Then you leave.'

'Don't be absurd.'

'I'm not the one being absurd,' she said coolly. 'Yes, I agree that the situation is far from ideal but I want this job. And you need an architect. The palace is falling apart and bullet holes are so last century.'

His jaw tightened. 'I don't mix business with pleasure.'

'Neither do I,' she fired back. 'Believe me, the last thing I'm looking for is a repeat of that afternoon.

'Nor am I.'

'Then I really don't see that there's anything to worry about.'

'Don't you?' he said, dropping his gaze and letting it slide over her body.

Heat began to pour over her. Desire flared to life but she banked it down. Right now her work was more important than anything else. She was *not* going to let it go. For anything.

'I,' she said pointedly, 'am perfectly capable of separating business and pleasure. I,' she added, 'should be able to control myself. Besides there is nothing you can do to make me go.'

His gaze dropped to her mouth and stayed there. His face darkened, his eyes took on a wicked gleam and Laura swallowed. Her heart lurched and a ball of nerves lodged in her throat. OK, so for all her fine words if Matt jumped to his feet, stalked round his desk, hauled her into his arms and kissed her she'd probably be through the door in seconds. But after loftily declaring that he didn't mix business with pleasure she had to hope he wouldn't put her to the test.

But why was he so desperate to get rid of her? Anyone would think she'd been stalking him. And what was all that hostility about? Surely he couldn't be *that* annoyed she'd run off?

'Look,' she said, 'you must be busy and the palace is huge. Our paths need never cross.' Thankfully.

Matt sighed, got to his feet and gave her one last glower before picking up his laptop. 'Just make sure you stay out of my way.'

CHAPTER SEVEN

THIS was getting ridiculous, Matt thought, struggling to pay attention to what his advisors were saying. He was in the middle of a discussion about the huge gaps in the public accounts and all he could think about was what Laura was up to.

He hadn't laid eyes on her in the two weeks since she'd been hired. Not that he'd been looking out for her especially. No. He'd had far too much to do. But it did seem odd. The palace might be big but it wasn't *that* large.

In a weird way her absence simply made him more aware of her presence. Which didn't make any sense at all.

Maybe it was the knowledge that he'd overreacted again and undoubtedly owed her another apology. Snapping at her like that to stay out of his way, snapping at anyone for that matter, wasn't how he chose to behave.

But then since he'd met her a lot of his behaviour had been uncharacteristic. If it carried on much longer his reputation for being tough and uncompromising would lie in tatters.

What was it about her that set him so on edge? Why did he have this niggling feeling that she was some kind of a threat? A threat to what exactly? In his experience threats came from rival bidders for a company he wanted and from despotic former presidents with their hands in the till. They did not come from curvy blond-haired blue-eyed architects.

Matt shoved his hands through his hair and let out a growl of frustration. Whatever the hell was going on, it couldn't continue.

He'd start with the apology. The sooner he got that out of the way, the better. And then he'd take the opportunity to find out a little more about her.

Something about the sabbatical she'd claimed she was on, the way she'd avoided his eyes when she'd mentioned it, had been gnawing at his brain. Whatever it was, she was working for him and he should get to the bottom of it.

And that was another thing, he realised suddenly. His company employed dozens of permanent staff and he'd always made a point of getting to know every one of them. Now Laura was on his payroll and what did he know about her? Apart from what she felt like in his arms and wrapped around him, precious little.

Matt ignored the bolt of heat that gripped his body and set his jaw. In fact that was probably what had been bothering him. The non-observation of formalities.

'Sir?'

He snapped his head round to his secretary who was sitting on his right and refocused his attention. 'What?' he said, and added a quick smile to mitigate the sharpness of his tone.

'I hope you don't mind my asking, but is everything all right?'

'Fine. What does Signorina Mackenzie do for lunch?'

The only indication that Antonio Capelli was surprised by a question about lunch in the midst of a conversation about corruption was a double blink. 'I believe she takes a sandwich to the rose garden.'

A sandwich? Matt's jaw tightened. No one could survive on a sandwich. 'What time?'

'One-ish, I believe. Would you like me to check?'

'No, that's fine. Where's the rose garden?'

'Past the kitchen gardens. Before the lake. There's a gate in the hedge.'

'Thank you.'

Matt made a move to get to his feet but Antonio leaned forwards and said, 'The advisors are waiting for your comments.'

About what? Oh, yes. Now that he'd fixed the Laura problem he snapped his attention back to the discussion with thankfully familiar ease. 'How much is missing?'

'Approximately fifty million,' said one of the finance advisors.

Pushing his chair back, he stood, planted his hands on the table and said, 'Trace the money. I suggest you start with Switzerland. When you find out who's responsible, arrest them.'

Laura finished off the last of her cheese sandwich and brushed the crumbs off her skirt. Breathing in the heady scent of roses, she sighed with pleasure. She'd stumbled on this little slice of heaven the day she'd arrived back with all her things, and, absolutely certain that it was one place Matt, or anyone else for that matter, would never visit, she'd made a habit of having lunch here, followed by half an hour of sunbathing before getting back to work.

The weather was gorgeous, the work was absorbing,

and Matt and his disturbing effect on her composure were nowhere to be seen. What could be better?

Laura stood up, unzipped her overalls and pushed them down to her waist. Then she lay down on the grass, closed her eyes as the sun hit her bare skin and basked in the warmth.

This was so the life…

She was in the middle of a particularly lovely daydream in which she was picking up a RIBA European award for her work on the palace when she heard the squeaking of the gate.

Her heart jumped. Her ears pricked. And caught another squeak. Swiftly followed by a sharp intake of breath and a muttered curse.

Her pulse racing, Laura jackknifed up. Grabbed the sides of her overalls and clutched them to her chest. She twisted round. And nearly passed out.

Matt was standing just inside the gate, frozen to the spot, staring down at her, his face set, but his eyes blazing.

Laura swallowed and felt a raging blush hit her cheeks. Too late to hope that he hadn't seen her semi-naked. OK, so she was at least wearing her bra, which was something to be thankful for, but the muscle hammering in his jaw and the tension in his body told her that he'd seen more than enough.

'You scared the life out of me,' she snapped, aiming for control by channelling her mortification into accusation.

'Next time I'll knock,' he said hoarsely, turning away so she could get her clothes in order.

'At least this time I'm not in danger of banging my head,' she muttered as she thrust her arms into the sleeves and whipped up the zip. Just passing out with overheating. Matt creeping up on her had better not become a habit.

Springing to her feet, Laura gave herself a quick shake and forced herself to calm down. 'You can turn round now,' she said lightly. 'I'm decent.'

More than decent, actually. Her nipples might be annoyingly as hard as pebbles, but the shapelessness of her overalls revealed nothing of the way her body responded to him, thank goodness.

Now all she had to do was sidle off, bury herself in work and find somewhere else to have lunch because, judging by the hamper hanging from his hand and banging against his knees, Matt had decided to appropriate this spot and frankly, with thousands of other heavenly spots in the grounds of the palace it wasn't really worth arguing over.

'Right. Well. I'll—er—leave you to it.'

'Don't go.' Matt flashed her a smile and her stomach flipped. Awareness whizzed through the entire length of her as, unable to help herself, she ran her gaze over every gorgeous inch of him, from the top of his thick dark hair right the way down, past the T-shirt and jeans down to the flip-flops.

She paused and blinked, not sure she'd heard him correctly. 'What?'

'My being here isn't exactly a coincidence.'

Laura frowned. 'Did you want something?'

'I came to see if you'd like some lunch.' He strode towards her and set the hamper beside the table.

'I've already had it.'

'Have some more.'

'I'm not hungry.'

'Fine, you can keep me company while I have lunch,'

he said, folding himself into the chair on the other side of the table and waving that she do the same.

Hmm. 'I need to get back to work.'

'Later.' He gave her a quick smile. 'Indulge me.'

Her stomach swooped. 'Do I have any option?'

'Not a lot,' he said, his eyes glinting with amusement and turning her head inside out. 'According to the records, disobeying the king used to result being thrown in the dungeon.'

'Charming.'

'Not in the least,' he said cheerfully. 'It's damp and crawling with vermin. You wouldn't like it.'

Probably not. Although she was pretty sure it would be less uncomfortable than having lunch with Matt when her common sense had gone AWOL. 'Wow,' she said, arching an eyebrow and crossing her arms. 'Absolute power and blackmail. That's quite a combination.'

'I like to think so.'

Laura tilted her head. 'I thought I was supposed to be staying out of your way.'

He glanced at her for a second and then grinned. 'That was one of the things I wanted to chat about.'

Now he wanted to chat? She narrowed her eyes. 'Don't you have better things to do? Like a country to run?'

'Even kings need to eat. And I thought we could get round to some of that small talk you mentioned.'

The small talk they'd been too busy getting horizontal and naked to bother with…

Laura's insides tangled into a mass of longing and frustration. Why was she always on the back foot with this man? What was it about him that had her feeling totally at sea? And more importantly why hadn't the two weeks she'd spent staying out of his way done anything to reduce the effect he had on her?

She nibbled on her lip. Maybe small talk *was* the way forward. If she could get him to reveal a bit about himself, maybe he'd turn out to be hideously arrogant, irritatingly patronising and possibly insanely boring. If she was really lucky, he'd also expose a couple of nasty habits. Like interrupting her. Or dismissing her opinions as if batting away a fly. As her ex had had a tendency to do. Hah. *That* would certainly put her off.

Laura sat down and gave him a cool smile. 'What would you like to talk about?'

Matt leaned down and took a bottle and a couple of glasses out of the hamper. 'It's occurred to me that the apologies I owe you are beginning to stack up.'

Oh. Damn. Not that hideously arrogant, then. She lifted a shoulder. 'Are they?'

He pulled the cork out, filled the glasses and slid one across the table to her. 'First of all, I never apologised for jumping to the conclusion you were a journalist.'

He'd made up for it in other ways, Laura thought, drawing the glass towards her, and then wished she hadn't as her cheeks went red.

'And then when you turned up here, I overreacted.'

She took a sip of wine and felt the alcohol slide into her stomach. 'Why?'

Matt frowned. 'I'm not sure.'

Hah. As if. She'd never met anyone less unsure of themselves. 'Let me guess,' she said with a flash of perception. 'You thought I was here to see you.' He stiffened and she felt a jolt of triumph. 'And I bet you thought the worst.'

'Possibly.'

'You really ought to do something about that suspicious nature of yours.'

'Perhaps.'

'Have lots of people crawled out of the woodwork now that you're king?'

His face tightened. 'Some.'

'Well, I don't know what sort of people you usually hang out with but you should look at getting a new set of friends.'

'You're probably right.' Matt sighed and then snapped back from wherever he'd been. 'So how am I doing?'

'Not bad.'

'Not bad?'

'Well, you haven't actually apologised yet.'

'Good point.' He frowned and shifted in the seat. 'I'm sorry.'

Laura couldn't help grinning at his obvious discomfort. 'Not a fan of apologising?'

Matt grimaced. 'I haven't had a huge amount of practice.'

Lucky him. She'd had years of practice. Often apologising for things that hadn't been her fault. God, she'd been pathetic. 'I dare say you'll get better at it.'

He winced. 'I don't plan on having to.'

'No, well, I doubt kings generally have much to apologise for.'

Didn't they? Any more of those sexy little smiles, thought Matt, and he'd be apologising for a whole lot more than a misunderstanding and an overreaction.

Because despite the shapeless mass of beige cotton covering Laura from head to toe, the imprint of her lying there on the grass in just her bra burned in his head and she might as well be naked. Every time she tucked her hair behind her ears or reached for her glass and lifted it to her mouth the thick cotton rustled and reminded him of exactly what lay beneath.

His head swam for a second and his hands curled into fists. Oh, for God's sake. He really had to get a grip.

Right. Conversation. That had been the plan. Food might not be a bad idea, either, he thought, taking out a couple of plates, cutlery and a number of small plastic boxes. He pushed a plate across the table to Laura but she shook her head. He opened the boxes and piled a selection of things on his plate.

'So how's the accommodation?' he asked.

See. He could do conversation.

'Very comfortable, thank you. Who could complain about a four-poster bed and marble en-suite?'

The image of Laura hot and naked and wet in the shower slammed into his head and his mouth went dry as the heavy beat of desire began to pound through him. Perhaps best to steer clear of accommodation as a conversational avenue in the future.

'And the work?'

'Really great,' she said, giving him a dazzling smile that nearly blinded him.

'You're very dedicated.' Neither his culture minister nor his secretary could stop singing her praises. It had been driving him insane.

'I love my job.'

'So why the sabbatical?'

Her glass froze halfway to her mouth and she carefully set it back down on the table. 'What do you mean?' she said warily.

'Well, you're clearly good at your job, and you said yourself you love it. So why the sabbatical?'

'Oh, well, you know.' She shrugged and nibbled on her lip in that way that he was discovering meant that she was nervous. Excellent. When he'd thought that something didn't add up he'd been right.

'I needed some time out. Stress. Boredom. That sort of thing.'

Matt didn't believe that for a second. Her whole demeanour had changed and if pushed he'd have said she looked downright shifty. 'You don't seem the type to suffer from stress or boredom.'

'Then I guess it's working.'

Hmm. Never mind. He'd get to the bottom of her sabbatical soon enough. 'How long have you lived in Little Somerford?'

She visibly relaxed. 'A couple of months.'

'And before that?'

'London. Born and bred.'

'Do you miss it?'

'Bits.'

'Which bits?'

'The theatres. My friends.'

Matt tilted his head. 'You must be what…late twenties?'

'Early thirties,' she said cagily, her eyes narrowing.

'And you move from the bright lights of London and a good job to hole up in a remote village in the country. Why?'

Laura studied her feet. 'I fancied a change of scenery.'

'During your sabbatical?' he said dryly.

'Exactly.'

'Aren't you quite young to take a sabbatical?'

Her head shot up and her eyes flashed. 'What's with this obsession with my sabbatical?'

Matt lifted his shoulders and gave her a smile. 'I'm just interested.'

Laura frowned. 'You should meet my friend Kate.'

'Why?'

'You both have persistence in spades,' she said darkly. 'You'd get on like a house on fire.'

Matt grinned. 'Persistence is useful in my line of work.'

'I'd call it nosiness.'

'That's useful, too. Bit risky, though, I'd have thought, to take a sabbatical at such a relatively early stage in your career.'

Laura let out an exasperated sigh and then threw her hands up. 'Fine,' she said, glaring at him. 'I didn't exactly choose to take a sabbatical. I was made redundant.'

'Ah,' Matt said, his mouth curving into a triumphant smile.

'There were cutbacks in government spending. Projects were axed. Heads rolled. Mine was one of them.'

'Ouch.' Whoever had employed her had been idiots for letting her go. But their loss, his gain. Or rather *Sassania's* gain, he amended swiftly.

She stared at him for a second, then blinked. 'Well, yes,' she said. 'But actually, not as ouch now as it was at the time.' She gave him a quick smile. 'In fact with the benefit of hindsight I ought to have sent them a big bunch of flowers to say thank you.'

'Why?' Matt wished she wouldn't do that blinking thing. It made him lose his train of thought. The colour of her eyes was so deep, so intense that when the blue disappeared he thought it a shame, yet when it reappeared his head swam and he wished she'd kept her eyes shut.

'If I hadn't been made redundant, I wouldn't have been free to take on this.' She waved an arm in the direction of the palace. 'I have ex-colleagues who would give their eye teeth to be here.'

Matt dragged his attention back to the conversation and hmmed. He doubted any of them would have her dedication or enthusiasm. 'That explains the "sabbatical",' he said, 'but why leave London?'

The wince was tiny but he caught it and something stabbed him in the chest. 'London gets a trifle dull after a while, don't you find?'

'No.'

'Oh.' She frowned. And then shrugged. 'Well, each to their own.'

Barriers were springing up all around her telling him to back off. But as she'd pointed out, he was persistent.

'I don't buy it,' he said, deceptively mildly.

'Tough.'

Matt leaned forwards. 'Tell me.'

'No.'

But she was wavering.

'Maybe I can help.'

'You already did,' she said, and then went bright red.

'How?'

'Doesn't matter.'

'If it involves me it does matter.'

'Let's just say I met you at a time when my self-esteem wasn't exactly sky-high.'

'And I boosted it?'

'Something like that,' she muttered.

'You used me.' Matt sat back and wondered whether he was hurt or amused.

Her gaze flew to his. 'No. Of course not.'

Oh, she was terrible at lying. He didn't say anything,

just lifted an eyebrow and stared at her until her cheeks went even redder.

'Well, maybe just a little bit.' She screwed up her eyes as if not wanting to see his reaction.

She needn't have worried. He had no complaints. 'Charming,' he said mildly, folding his arms over his chest and grinning. 'I'm devastated.'

Her eyes flew open in shock and then she relaxed and returned his grin. 'I can tell.'

'Nevertheless, I think you owe me an explanation.'

'I don't see why. Can you honestly say you didn't use me?'

'This isn't about me.'

Laura nodded and took a deep breath. 'OK, fine. The day I was made redundant I got home early to find my boyfriend at the time with his secretary. In our bed.'

'Ah.'

'I know. Tacky, or what? They'd been having an affair for three months, would you believe, and I hadn't a clue. I'd rented my flat out when I moved in with him and, what with three being a bit of a crowd, I couldn't exactly stick around. So I trawled through the websites of a number of rental agencies and found the cottage in Little Somerford and I left.'

'What a jerk.' The hammering urge to hunt her ex-boyfriend down and pummel the living daylights out of him thumped Matt in the chest, taking him completely by surprise.

She blinked. 'Well, yes. But I guess he wasn't wholly to blame.'

'Seems to me that that kind of behaviour is inexcusable,' he muttered, wondering exactly where such a violent reaction had come from.

She bit her lip. 'True, but I was too easy-going, too

easy to please. Too afraid of confrontation. I let him get away with too much. I let him walk all over me.' She shrugged.

Easy-going? Afraid of confrontation? Matt nearly fell off his chair. That didn't sound like the Laura he knew. Since the moment he'd met her she'd been feisty, fearless and determined.

Snapshots flew around his head. Of Laura on the path, batting her eyelids and pouting. Arching her back on his sofa and staring up at him with that come-hither look. Sitting in his office, limbs crossed, chin up as she told him she wasn't leaving.

His stomach churned with a weird combination of lust, admiration and something that felt suspiciously like jealousy.

'Which has kind of been the story of my life,' she was saying. 'Much as it pains me to admit it, I have been a bit of a doormat.'

Matt dragged himself back to the conversation. 'You could have fooled me,' he muttered, his voice not betraying any hint of the confusion battering his brain.

Laura grinned. 'Ah, well, that's because after the double whammy of losing my job and my boyfriend I went on an assertiveness course.'

'That sounds dangerous.'

'It was. Very. Module One was entitled "How to Embrace Confrontation". Module Two covered learning how to say no. And Module Three focused on how to get what you want.'

'You must be a fast learner.'

Laura nodded. 'Like lightning.'

'For someone allegedly afraid of confrontation,' he said dryly, 'you're pretty good at it.'

She grinned and his stomach swooped. 'It's turned

out to be surprisingly liberating. As has going for what I want and saying no.'

Sometimes saying no wasn't all it was cracked up to be. Sometimes the only word a man wanted to hear was yes. In exactly the breathy pleading way she'd said all those little yeses that afternoon.

'Anyway. Change is good, don't you think?'

'Depends on the change,' Matt muttered, struggling to keep his focus on reconciling the Laura he knew to the one she described and not on the yeses. 'Where did the pushover tendencies come from?'

'My parents' divorce when I was thirteen, I suppose.'

'Tricky.'

'Very.'

'Amicable?'

She winced. 'Hideous.'

'I'm sorry.'

Laura shrugged. 'Things had been bad for years, even though at the time it all seemed so sudden. I think I probably compensated by trying not to put a foot wrong, in the childish hope that if I was good enough they'd stay together. Which was nuts, of course,' she said. 'I know it had nothing to do with me and they're far happier apart, but I guess old habits die hard.'

'If ever.'

Laura shook her head. 'Ah, you see, that's where you're wrong. My people-pleasing days are well and truly over.'

That was a shame.

The thought slammed into Matt's head before he could stop it and stayed there flashing in neon, reminding him just how well she'd pleased him.

'Anyway why the sudden interest?'

Matt shrugged and shoved the thought aside. 'I'm interested in all my members of staff.'

For a second there was an odd sort of stunned silence. Laura's face paled and Matt felt a chill suddenly run through him as if the sun had disappeared behind a cloud.

She blinked. Bit on her lip. Nodded slowly. 'Of course,' she said in a strangely soft voice, getting to her feet a little jerkily. 'Right.' She nodded again. Ran her hands over her hips, pulled her shoulders back and flashed him an overly bright smile. 'Well, as a member of staff, and a brand-new one at that, I ought to be getting back to work. Thank you for the wine.'

Before Matt could ask her what the matter was, Laura had spun on her heel and was stalking off in the direction of the hedge as if she couldn't get away fast enough.

He watched her disappear through the gate, bewilderment pummelling at his brain. What the hell was all that about? Matt rubbed his face. He'd thought their conversation had been going swimmingly. He'd got to the bottom of her sabbatical and was just beginning to discover what made her tick. And even more surprisingly, he'd found himself enjoying her company.

So what had happened? Had he said something? Done something?

God. He swore softly under his breath. He was famed for being decisive, intuitive, shrewd and for having a certain ruthlessness that had made him a billionaire by the time he was thirty. He'd built up a multimillion-pound business from scratch. He'd negotiated impossible deals and turned the most desperate of companies around. Now he was running a country with every problem going.

Yet he'd never understand women. They were completely unfathomable.

Even Alicia, who'd been so transparent and straightforward, had eventually become incomprehensible. Matt's jaw tightened as the memory of his ex-fiancée filtered into his head. Her lack of guile had been one of the reasons he'd asked her to marry him. She hadn't tried to wrap him up in complex emotional games. Their relationship had been easy, light and fun.

Until he'd started to get more caught up with his business. As it had grown he'd had to devote more and more time to it and less to her.

At first she'd been remarkably stoical, supportive even, but even the most understanding fiancée would have got fed up eventually.

Matt had been torn, and while the relationship limped on for a while it hadn't survived. The end had been messy and painful. Hurtful accusations had flown all over the place. Guilt and blame had built and built, until things had finally erupted. The only thing that had kept him sane during and after their break-up had been his work.

Now he avoided relationships like the plague. They were perplexing, unpredictable and ultimately emotionally destructive, and he never wanted to go through all that again.

Matt set his jaw and put everything back into the hamper. Laura was perplexing, unpredictable and he had a horrible suspicion she could be pretty emotionally destructive.

So there'd be no more seeking her out, he thought, getting to his feet and heading back to the palace. No more lunches. No more conversation. And definitely no more wanting her in his bed.

When their paths crossed he'd be cool and distant. Because he was far better off alone. Always had been, always would be.

Staff, thought Laura for the billionth time that afternoon. Huh.

Disappointment and hurt scythed through her all over again and she threw down her chisel before she could do any permanent damage to the frieze she was working on.

God. How stupid could she be? If only she were wearing steel-capped boots she could have given herself the kicking she deserved. Because she was such an idiot.

She closed her eyes for a second and felt her cheeks burn as her mind hurtled back to the rose garden. There she'd been, going all soft and squidgy and mellowing with the wine and the sun and the heat of Matt's gaze. Bizarrely she'd found herself enjoying the conversation despite it dredging up things she'd rather not think about. It had actually been a relief to talk about the old her, and she'd discovered she rather liked the person she was beginning to become.

Unfortunately there hadn't been a hint of arrogance, nor a patronising glance in sight. And while Matt had been annoyingly persistent he hadn't interrupted her and he hadn't dismissed anything she'd said. In fact the way his body had tensed and his eyes had blazed when she'd told him about her ex had had her heart leaping with something she wasn't sure she wanted to identify and desire whipping through her so fiercely that she'd begun to wonder why exactly business and pleasure shouldn't mix.

And all the time he'd just been interrogating her as he would any employee.

Agh. Laura opened her eyes and scowled. The fact that she was still smarting over it two hours later was infuriating. And what was making things worse was the knowledge that she didn't have any real reason to smart. Which irritated her even further.

Because Matt was right. She was staff.

So what was she getting so het up about?

Laura plonked herself on the floor and chewed her lip. Was it really the fact that he'd wangled so much personal information out of her without divulging even his age, which was what she'd been telling herself for the past hour or so?

Or was it actually the fact that she'd spent the entire conversation on the point of combusting while Matt had sat there, ice cool and controlled and totally indifferent?

As the heat and desire that were never far away flared to life and started zooming around her body, Laura swallowed. Well, that cleared that up, she thought, hauling herself out of denial and sticking her chin in her hands.

She might as well admit it. For all the decisions she'd made, all the self-analysis she'd done, all the stern talking-tos she'd given herself, she was finding it increasingly difficult to remember exactly why she wasn't leaping into Matt's arms and tumbling him into bed.

Whereas he, on the other hand, appeared to have forgotten that that mad passionate afternoon in his house had ever taken place.

Huh. Talk about unflattering.

Laura frowned and her mind raced. She'd had enough of constantly flailing around for control while Matt remained the epitome of cool. Wasn't it about time she redressed the balance? Wouldn't it be interesting to see if she couldn't shake him up a bit and get him on the wrong foot for a change?

Her heart began to hammer and her stomach buzzed with adrenalin. Yes. Why the hell not? And tonight, at the party she'd heard Matt was hosting, would be the ideal occasion.

She hadn't been invited. He wouldn't be expecting her. She had a killer dress and shoes that made her feel a million dollars.

What could be more perfect?

CHAPTER EIGHT

MATT had had the event this evening arranged to evaluate the country's entrepreneurial spirit and ascertain the existing barriers to business. He'd had invitations sent out to five hundred of Sassania's most innovative and exciting entrepreneurs and the ballroom was now filled with a buzz that gave him more satisfaction than he'd have ever imagined.

So far the evening had been going splendidly. He'd had a number of extremely worthwhile conversations, and had gained a valuable insight into the way to kick-start the economy and stimulate growth.

After all the political problems he'd had to deal with recently, not to mention the unsettling effect Laura had on him, spending an evening within his comfort zone made a nice change.

As did the way he now felt, or rather didn't feel, about Laura. After she'd left him in the rose garden, he'd gone back to his office, summoned up some of that famed ruthlessness and had simply told himself to get a grip and not to feel anything.

So he didn't. When she crossed his mind, he felt absolutely nothing. Not a flicker of desire. Not a hammer of his pulse. Not a twitch of his body. The abrupt way in which she'd left him after lunch? Hah. Didn't bother him one jot.

Laura, metaphorically speaking, was history, and he hadn't been so relaxed in weeks.

Striding over to the podium and adjusting the microphone, Matt felt an exquisite sense of calm settle over him. Oh, yes. He was back on track and back in control. And nothing, but nothing, could upset it.

Laura hovered at the pair of giant doors that opened into the ballroom, her gaze zooming in on the man standing on the podium speaking to the assembled throng, and her breath caught.

Matt looked absolutely magnificent. Dark and dangerous and devastatingly gorgeous. His dinner suit fitted as if made for him and the snowy white of his shirt emphasised his tan. The aura he emanated and the magnetism he radiated were holding every one of his guests captivated.

God, she'd only just arrived and hadn't heard any of his speech, yet *she* was captivated. Her eyes slid helplessly back to him and her blood began to heat. Who knew what he was talking about? She was far too distracted by the hint of a smile curving his mouth and the sexy raise of an eyebrow he gave every now and then. Every inch of him seemed to reach out to her and she was moments away from discarding all her intentions of lofty hauteur, and swooning.

A woman to her right let out a little sigh and Laura felt like going over and patting her arm in sympathy. And then batting everyone out of the way, stalking over and staking her claim on him.

Her totally unfounded claim, she reminded herself, biting her tongue and forcing herself to focus.

'Small businesses are the backbone to any economy,' Matt was saying, his gaze sweeping over the assembled gathering, 'and I plan to see that measures are implemented to—'

His eyes collided with hers and for a second, time stood still. He paused. His face tightened. His eyes blazed and Laura's heart skidded to a halt. Her mouth went dry. Her entire body froze and then burned as awareness sizzled through her.

And then Matt continued his sweep of the room as if nothing had happened and time set off again.

'—to encourage their development. Thank you.'

Applause rumbled around her as Matt stepped down, but Laura barely registered it. She could hardly breathe with the nerves that were suddenly attacking her from all sides.

Oh, God, she thought, struggling not to sag against the door. This had been *such* a bad idea. Because for that brief moment Matt had not looked happy to see her. In fact he'd looked downright furious.

Her heart tumbled. How had she ever thought she could get the upper hand with a man like him? He was a king, for heaven's sake. A natural born leader. He was alpha through and through, whereas she had spent her whole life sitting squarely at the omega end of the scale. OK, so she might be inching up that particular alphabet but still she was in way over her head.

What the hell had she been thinking? What had given her the nerve to presume she could shake him up? Come to think of it, why on earth would she want to shake him up anyway? Shaking Matt up would be like rattling a lion's cage while leaving the gate open. Had she gone completely nuts?

Laura's heart began to race. She ought to leave. Pretend she'd never come. Now.

But with Antonio Capelli striding towards her, smiling warmly in welcome and taking her elbow, it was far too late to flee.

Oh, *hell,* thought Matt, plucking a glass of champagne off the tray of a passing waiter and forcing himself not to down it in one.

What was Laura doing here? He deliberately hadn't invited her so he must have done something truly horrendous in a past life to deserve this kind of torment, he thought grimly, gripping the glass and muttering some sort of appropriate response to the question he was being asked.

When his gaze had skated over the room and landed on her, everything had seemed to judder to a halt. His heart had thumped and for a split second his head had gone blank. He'd forgotten where he was, what he was doing and more worryingly what he was supposed to be saying.

It had taken every ounce of strength he possessed to drag his gaze from hers and continue his perusal of the room. With every fibre of his being suddenly on fire what he'd really wanted to do was leap off the podium, shove everyone out of the way and drag her off somewhere private.

So much for his famed ruthlessness. He could only hope to God that no one had noticed him falter.

Matt felt his eyes narrow as he watched Laura being wheeled off by his secretary and suspicion began to wind through him. If Antonio had had anything to do with Laura's presence at the party he could well be finding a new job come the morning.

But never mind, he told himself as they disappeared into the melee. There were five hundred people in the room and there was absolutely no reason why he'd even need to go up to her, let alone have to speak to her.

All he had to do was forget she was there and everything would be fine.

Forgetting Laura was at the party was easier said than done, Matt thought, an agonising hour later.

He might not have had any need to approach her, but that didn't stop him being aware of every move she made. It didn't stop him subconsciously manoeuvring himself towards her, and it didn't stop him wanting to march over and throw out any man she spoke to, smiled at or laughed with. Of which there were far too many.

Running a finger around the inside of his collar, Matt felt uncomfortably hot and weirdly on edge. His muscles actually ached with the effort of keeping his body where it was and his brain hurt with the effort of concentrating on the conversations going on around him.

Unable to help himself, he glanced over to where she was chatting and smiling, her eyes sparkling and her cheeks pink. He caught her eye. She arched an eyebrow, as if she was well aware he was avoiding her, and something inside him snapped.

This was absurd. Trying to ignore her wasn't working. Why the hell shouldn't he just go over and say hello? That wouldn't kill him, would it?

Gritting his teeth, Matt excused himself and started to make his way over to her.

Which wasn't as easy as it sounded. She was standing only a few metres away, but she might as well have been in a different country. To his intense frustration people kept coming up to him like heat-seeking missiles. Interrupting his trajectory and wanting to have a word.

By the time he finally made it to her, he'd agreed to a dozen things he probably shouldn't have, and his already stretched-to-the-limit patience was dangerously close to snapping.

It wasn't helped by the lifted chin or the cool haughty smile she greeted him with. Or the long strapless blue dress she was wearing that matched her eyes and clung everywhere. Did she have *any* idea how little it left to the imagination?

Matt thrust his hands in his pockets. 'Good evening,' he said, his tone far sharper than he'd have liked.

'Your Majesty,' she said, dropping into a graceful curtsey.

What the hell? Matt ground his teeth. 'Don't do that.'

She rose and gave him a smile that had his heart pounding. 'Am I doing it wrong?'

'No.' She did it very well. Sank so low that he could see straight down the front of her dress. 'But don't do it again. Not you.'

She sighed dramatically and pouted. 'And I spent such a long time practising.'

Matt blinked and tried to keep his eyes out of her cleavage and some sort of grip on his control. 'What are you doing here?'

'I thought it might be a good idea to see how the ballroom works. From a restoration perspective.'

'Gatecrashing?'

'Not at all,' said Laura coolly. 'Once I explained my intentions to Signore Capelli, he added me to the guest list.'

Hah. As he'd thought. He'd definitely be having words with his secretary.

'Nice dress.' His voice sounded strangely hoarse and he cleared his throat.

'Thank you. Nice suit.'

'Thank you.'

She tilted her head back to take a sip of her champagne and Matt's gaze dropped to her throat. Soft and creamy skin. Completely exposed. He curled his hands into fists deep in his pockets to stop himself reaching out, pulling her against him and setting his mouth to the pulse thumping at the base of her neck.

Then she lowered her glass and shot him a languid look and a smouldering smile that set his body on fire. 'Are you all right, Matt?'

He pulled himself together. 'Fine. Why?'

'You look a little uncomfortable.'

'Just a trifle warm.'

'So why are you glowering? This is a party. You shouldn't be glowering.'

'It's my party. I can do whatever I like.'

Her smile deepened. Turned faintly knowing, and Matt's pulse hammered. Would anyone notice if he hauled her away somewhere private to continue the party alone?

'Well, you must be busy,' she said, her voice unusually husky. 'Don't let me keep you.'

'You aren't.'

'Great speech.'

Had it been? He couldn't remember. Her gaze shimmered at him with something he couldn't identify but made desire pound through him.

Matt's head swam. What on earth had got into her

tonight? Where had this sultry hauteur sprung from? And what was he going to do about it?

'This is a lovely room,' she said, looking up and giving him another view of her throat.

'I don't want to talk about the room,' he grated.

If she was surprised by his tone, she didn't show it. In fact her eyes began to sparkle with something that looked suspiciously like triumph. Which only wound him up further. 'Then what do you want to talk about?'

He didn't want to talk at all. 'Why did you dash off like that earlier?' he said, drawing on the first thing that sprang to mind.

Laura lifted her shoulders and Matt had to force himself not to glance down. 'Things to do.'

His eyes narrowed. 'Running away from me seems to be becoming a habit.'

'Not at all. You simply reminded me of my place, that's all.'

Matt frowned. What the hell did that mean? Her place was in his arms. Beneath him. On top of him. Whichever way, plastered against him was where she should be.

His jaw clenched as the desire pounding through him grew hotter, more insistent.

He'd had enough of this. Enough of the eyelash batting and the sultry little smiles. Enough of the hammering desire and tight tension keeping him awake all night and ruining his concentration all day. Enough of trying to resist her.

For whatever reason, Laura was in a dangerous mood tonight and, despite his best efforts to hang on to it, Matt's control was slipping away like sand through an hourglass. He'd never felt such a need clawing at his gut.

Never felt such desperation. Never had so little desire for conversation.

To hell with the entrepreneurs. He'd done plenty to ease their concerns. Now it was his turn.

Stepping forward, Matt took her elbow and pulled her against him.

'What are you doing?' Laura muttered, her breath catching.

'We're leaving,' he said as the scent of her spun into his head and obliterated all rational thought.

'We can't.'

'We can and we are.'

She glanced up at him, a tiny frown creasing her brow. 'Is something wrong?'

'Very.'

'What is it?'

Out of the corner of his eye Matt caught the flash of movement, a glimpse of someone heading over to talk to him. Oh, no. No way. 'Have you seen the Sala dell'Anticollegio yet?' he said loudly, wheeling her off in the opposite direction and not giving her time to answer. 'Incredible vaulted ceiling. Badly in need of some TLC.' As was he.

So much for lofty hauteur, thought Laura, tottering alongside Matt in her three inch stilettos.

It had all been going so well. She'd been cool and collected and she'd been enjoying the party hugely. Well, as much as anyone burning up with longing could.

She'd felt Matt's eyes on her the entire evening, making her heart thump with a weird kind of anticipation and her body tingle. How she'd managed to hold any kind of sensible conversation was a miracle. At one point she'd even let out a low groan and had had to quickly turn it into a cough, which had been mortifying.

But by and large she'd kept herself under control.

Until Matt had started to make his way over and her self-possession had begun to slip away like silk over skin.

The closer he'd got, the harder she'd found it to move. Her feet seemed to have taken root. She'd lost track of the conversation going on around her. All she'd been aware of was Matt heading towards her, his expression turning grimmer by the second as yet another person engaged him in conversation, until he'd finally stopped in front of her, vibrating with an electric kind of tension that had her entire body buzzing.

And all she'd been able to think was who exactly was meant to be shaking up whom?

He ushered her through the doors and across the hall. He opened the door opposite, practically pushed her in, followed her and then closed it behind him. At the sudden silence after the vibrant noise of the party the edginess winding through her tripled. Her heart hammered and a flutter of nerves clutched at her stomach.

'Did you really bring me here to look at the ceiling?' she said, her voice sounding thick and husky and totally unlike hers.

'What do you think?' Matt's eyes glittered as he moved past her and switched on the table lamp. Soft golden light bathed the room and Laura glanced up.

'I think it isn't vaulted and doesn't need any restoration.'

The glimmer of a smile played at his lips. 'So I lied.'

'Tut tut.'

Matt turned, shoved his hands in his pockets and

stared at her until her bones began to melt. 'You wanted to know what was wrong.'

Had she? When? Oh, yes. Just before the madness had taken over. 'I did,' she said, fervently hoping he wasn't going to launch into an attack on her work or something.

'You're what's wrong.'

Her heart lurched. 'Me?' That was almost as bad.

'You.'

'Why?'

'You drive me to distraction.'

Oh. Laura went dizzy for a second with the lust that shot through her. And then the knowledge that she'd been completely and utterly hoist by her own petard slammed into her. For a second the room spun. Shock ricocheted right through her. Swiftly followed by a deluge of relief and then everything suddenly fell into place.

She'd tried and tried to deny her attraction to Matt and she was sick of it. Sick of feeling constantly on edge and jumpy. She wanted Matt. So badly. And it seemed he wanted her, too.

The realisation was too much to resist and beneath the heat of his gaze the fragile barriers she'd tried to erect to protect herself came crashing down. What harm could just once more do? 'Well, that goes both ways.'

'Does it?' he murmured, his gaze dropping to her mouth.

'Oh, yes.'

Matt tilted his head. 'So what do you think we should do about it?'

She knew exactly what she wanted to do about it, but the whole bump-on-the-head/kiss misunderstanding that afternoon in his house suddenly flew into her head and made her pause. 'What do *you* think?'

'I think we should get it out of our systems.' He took a step towards her, his eyes gleaming, and her pulse thudded.

What an excellent idea. 'How?'

'You know perfectly well how.'

Her heart began to gallop. 'I thought you didn't mix business with pleasure.'

'I don't.'

'So what's this?'

'I don't employ you. The state does.'

Thank heavens for that. 'Good point. So when do you think we should set about getting it out of our systems?'

'What's wrong with now?'

Thrills scurried through her. 'There are hundreds of people on the other side of the corridor,' she said a little breathlessly.

'I locked the door,' he said, taking another step towards her.

'Won't you be missed?'

'I doubt it.' His eyes glittered as he stared down at her. 'I, on the other hand, have really missed this.'

Matt closed the short distance between them took her in his arms, bent his head and dropped a kiss on the skin where her neck met her shoulder. Her whole body jerked as if she'd been branded.

'Oh, God, so have I,' she said, feeling her knees begin to buckle as the last tiny remnant of her resistance crumbled.

As Matt slid his mouth up her neck Laura felt herself melt against him and clutched at his shoulders.

'You look amazing. You feel amazing,' he breathed against her jaw.

So did he. A tremble ran through her. 'This is insane,' she murmured.

'I know.'

Matt's mouth found hers and captured it in a slow scorching kiss that frazzled her brain. Laura moaned. Wound her fingers through his hair and pressed herself closer. She felt him slip his hands down her body and she began to burn.

And then went cold when Matt suddenly stopped and swore softly. 'What?' she said as disappointment thundered through her. Surely he couldn't be having second thoughts? Not now.

'You're not wearing any underwear.'

The disappointment vanished beneath a flood of relief. 'Clingy dress.'

And then she couldn't say anything more even if she'd wanted to because Matt had slammed his mouth down on hers and was backing her up against the nearest wall and pinning her against it with his hips, one hand in her hair, the other on her breast.

Feeling desperation begin to take hold, Laura delved beneath his jacket, tugged at his shirt and pulled it from the waistband of his trousers. She ran her fingers over the skin of his back and felt a shudder rip through him. Unable to help herself, she pressed harder against the steely length of his erection and rubbed against it.

And then he was pushing her dress up, sliding a hand round to where she was hot and wet and aching, and pressing the heel of his palm against her.

Laura shook with need as she fumbled with the button of his trousers. She yanked the zip down, ran her hand over him and urged him towards her. Matt let out a rough groan, then put a hand over hers and pulled back.

She blinked. What now?

'Don't,' he said, his voice tight with barely restrained need.

'Why not?'

'Because if this is going to go any further we need to go upstairs to my room and I won't be able to walk.'

'Why do we need to go upstairs?' said Laura, not caring that she sounded desperate. 'I don't need a bed. I'm perfectly happy with a wall.'

'And an unplanned pregnancy?' Matt said, his eyes blazing down at her as he stepped back.

'Oh.' Laura bit her lip and tugged her dress down. An unplanned pregnancy was the last thing she needed. But still… 'God, I wish I was irresponsible.'

'So do I,' he said, adjusting his clothing. 'But luckily we don't have to be, because upstairs I have condoms.' Taking her hand, Matt marched her across the room, unlocked the door and flung it open.

And came face to face with Signore Capelli, who was standing there, his hand raised as if about to knock.

Laura's heart banged in shock. And then lurched with something else when Matt dropped her hand as if it were a hot coal and sprang away from her. She glanced at him. Saw his face had turned to stone. Then she glanced at Signore Capelli who was decidedly not looking at her, and she felt herself grow beetroot at the thought of the damage Matt's hands must have done to her hair. What must he be thinking?

'Yes?' Matt growled.

'I apologise for disturbing you, sir,' said Signore Capelli, looking cool and unperturbed, as if he encountered this sort of situation all the time, 'but you're needed in the ballroom.'

Matt shoved his hands through his hair and bit out a sigh. Then he turned to Laura, his eyes blazing. 'Stay here,' he said. 'I'll be right back.'

But by the time Matt got back, Laura had gone.

CHAPTER NINE

LAURA was cursing Matt beneath her breath and punching the pillows on her bed when the hairs on the back of her neck sprang to attention and alerted her to the fact that she wasn't alone. Her heart suddenly thundering, she whirled around and nearly swooned.

Matt stood in the doorway, his big body tight with tension and his eyes glittering. His bow tie hung loose around his neck and a couple of his shirt buttons were undone. He looked dishevelled, exhausted and utterly gorgeous.

'I asked you to wait,' he said roughly.

What did he have to sound annoyed about? Laura thought, her stomach churning with pique, frustration and disappointment. She was the one who'd been left hanging there. Waiting. Listening to the heavy tick-tock of the grandfather clock and going slowly insane. 'Don't you ever knock?'

'No.'

'You should. It's rude.'

'I asked you to wait. You left. I don't think you should be lecturing me on rudeness.' His eyes glittered. 'What happened? Changed your mind?'

As if. She clutched a pillow to her stomach as if it might somehow provide some kind of defence against his potent magnetism. 'I did wait,' said Laura witheringly. 'For over an hour.'

There was a brief silence. Then Matt frowned. 'It wasn't as long as that.'

'Yes, it was.' Obviously he'd been so caught up in whatever it was he'd been doing that he'd completely forgotten about her. Exactly as she'd suspected.

'Oh,' he muttered, rubbing his face. 'I'm sorry, I got tied up.'

'Evidently,' she said waspishly, the hurt still stinging. 'So what do you want?'

His gaze dropped to her chest, where she was pretty sure he'd be able to see the curve of her breasts beneath the fine silk of her negligee and she tossed the pillow onto the bed to cross her arms over her chest.

'What do you think?' he said, stepping into the room, his eyes darkening. 'We have unfinished business.'

Her gaze dropped to below his belt and her mouth went dry at the impressive bulge behind the zip. Laura gave herself a quick shake, swallowed hard and lifted her chin. 'No, we don't.' She arched an eyebrow. Gave him a smile. 'At least *I* don't.' The minute she'd got to her suite, she'd stripped, marched into the bathroom and had had a hot, steamy, extremely satisfying shower. Steam and the scent of roses still billowed from room. Her cheeks were still pink. Her body still hummed.

For a second Matt just stared at her as the implication of her words sank in and his eyebrows crept up. 'Oh,' he said softly, giving her a slow smile that made her tingle all over again. 'I'm sorry I missed that.'

'So am I.'

'We'll just have to start again. Because look what I found.'

He strode across the marble floor, stopped a foot from

her and tossed a box onto the bed. Out spilled condoms. Lots of them. Laura stared down at them, back up at him and her pulse began to race.

'Oh.'

'Quite.' And then he frowned. '*Did* you change your mind?'

He sounded uncertain all of a sudden and pique evaporated. 'Of course not,' she said, giving him a smile that she hoped didn't reveal her relief too much. 'I just got bored of waiting.'

'Good.' Matt pulled her into his arms. 'Now where were we?' he said, staring down at her and a wicked smile curving his mouth. 'Oh, yes, I remember.'

He slid his hands down her body, bunched the silk in his fingers and lifted it. Laura raised her arms and let her bare breasts brush against his chest as he drew it up and over her head. She heard him take a sharp breath, then felt him give her shoulders a little push and she fell back on the bed.

Her breath shot from her lungs as she landed and then vanished all over again as Matt began to whip his clothes off. He pulled off his bow tie and tossed it on the floor. Seconds later his jacket and shirt joined it, followed by his trousers and shorts, and desire began to hammer through her.

Oh, God. His body was truly magnificent. The first time they'd had sex she'd been so desperate that there hadn't been time to savour and learn. And then up against the wall earlier this evening she'd barely had time to reacquaint herself with it.

But that was going to change, she vowed, her head swimming as she ran her gaze down him, over the broad chest, the flat stomach, lean hips, powerful thighs and finally lingering on the gloriously thick hard length of his erection.

Laura swallowed and shuddered as a bolt of longing gripped her. This time they'd take it slowly. Touch and taste and linger and eke out every drop of pleasure.

'Are you ogling me?' Matt murmured and Laura realised he'd been standing there watching her watching him for goodness knew how long.

'Certainly am,' she replied, biting on her lip to stop herself from whimpering.

He looked down at her, his eyes gleaming as they roamed over her.

'What are you doing?' she breathed, half wondering why he wasn't launching himself at her.

'Returning the compliment.'

Her body burned and she dragged in a shaky breath. 'Oh, OK.'

'Of course,' he mused, sinking onto the bed beside her and trailing his fingers over her cheek, down her neck, over her upper chest and then cupping her breast. 'It would be better if I had a pair of binoculars.'

Laura shivered and felt the muscles of her abdomen contract. 'Would it? Why?'

'Then I could ogle you from behind the curtains the way you were ogling me.'

'I was not ogling you,' she said weakly, swallowing and trying not to drown in the pleasure shooting through her.

'You were watching me for half an hour,' he murmured.

'Five minutes. At the most.'

'Fifteen. At the least.'

Laura sighed and closed her eyes and gave in. 'Well,

if you will insist on going around without your shirt on, what do you expect?'

'I was in my own garden,' he said against her ear. 'I have every right to go around without my shirt on. Or anything if I feel like it,' he added, dropping a trail of kisses along her jaw.

Lust began to pound through her. 'That's true.'

'I'd never have you pegged as a voyeur,' he muttered, his mouth moving lower, dropping a trail of kisses down her neck and over the top of her breasts. 'Who knew?'

'So arrest me.'

She gasped as his mouth closed over her nipple. Pleasure spun through her, arrowing down straight to the centre of her, and for a second she lost all track of the conversation.

He lifted his head. 'I would if I could remember where I put my handcuffs,' he said, switching his attention to her other breast.

Laura's entire body began to buzz and desire hammered at her with an insistence that demanded attention. Oh, forget slow and sensual. She just wanted him thrusting inside her. Right now.

Wrapping a leg around his calves, she urged him up, wound her arms around his neck and kissed him hard and deep. Tilted her hips and ground them against him, desperate for release. The shower had been good, but now she wanted the real thing.

Matt, however, clearly had other ideas. He lifted his head, breathing raggedly, his eyes blazing. 'What's the hurry?' he murmured.

What was the hurry? Laura bit her lip. She was on the point of exploding. That was the hurry. And then mortification swept down to mingle with the desire pummelling through her and she forced herself back under control.

'No hurry,' she managed thickly. 'I just thought, you know, you might be uncomfortable. In pain. Or something.'

'So altruistic.'

'That's me. Always thinking of others.'

'I hope not,' Matt said, lifting an eyebrow. 'I don't want you to be thinking about anyone but me.'

'Ah,' she said. 'Well, that's up to you.'

Matt's eyes flashed. 'Is that a challenge?'

'Maybe.'

'I like challenges.'

'Excellent,' she breathed and sighed with delight as he shifted down her body, spread her legs and settled himself between her thighs. At the touch of his mouth at her molten centre, she nearly leapt off the bed.

Oh, God. Forget thinking about anyone else. Forget thinking full stop. At the sheer force of the pleasure shooting through her, her brain shut down. Every drop of her conscious thought zoomed in on his mouth, his lips, his tongue and what they were doing to her.

Her heart thundered. Her hands clutched at the sheets and then tangled in his hair. She lifted her hips, couldn't stop her back arching as all the pleasure churning around inside her sharpened, shot to her core and then splintered.

Laura cried out as she broke apart. Felt a sob rise in her throat as Matt gripped her hips, tormenting her still further, sucking and licking at her, drawing out every tiny drop of pleasure as shudders continued to rack her body.

Matt moved up her, covering her still quivery body

entirely with his. 'Still thinking of others?' he muttered, his eyes blazing as they bore into hers.

Laura couldn't speak, just shook her head.

'Good.' And then a wicked gleam lit the depths of his eyes. 'Maybe I'd better make sure, just in case.'

Oh, God. Could she take any more? Surely it wasn't possible. Surely her body needed time to recover? But already she could feel herself softening and ripening and humming with renewed desire. 'That might be wise,' she said, finally regaining the power of speech, albeit a soft and breathy one.

'I'm delighted you agree.'

His mouth found hers and as he kissed her he stroked a hand down her body, over the damp triangle of curls at the juncture of her legs and slid a finger deep inside her.

Laura gasped into his kiss and felt herself clench around him.

'Unbelievable,' he muttered against her mouth.

'Incredible,' she panted.

'That, too.'

As he stroked her waves of pleasure began to roll over her. Unable to resist, she lifted her hips and pressed herself harder against him. Her breathing shallowed. Sped up. A ball of tension swelled and tightened inside her. Her heart thundered.

She felt Matt reach over, faintly heard the rustle of foil and then he was on top of her, pushing her knees even farther apart and driving into her.

Laura groaned in desperation. Her legs wrapped around his waist, pulling him farther inside her, and her hands tangled in his hair.

With every thrust of his body, every scorching kiss, he pushed her higher. Mindless with need, Laura tilted her hips to take him deeper. She could feel the tension in him too, the focus, as he pounded harder and faster into her.

And then just when she thought she couldn't bear the clawing desperation any longer, he pulled out of her and drove into her one last time, deeper than he had ever before.

Laura shattered. A tidal wave of pure pleasure crashed over her as her orgasm hit and rippled out along every single one of her nerve endings. A second later Matt let out a rough groan and collapsed on top of her.

As she floated back down to earth she became aware of his heart thundering against hers, his breath harsh and fast against her neck, and something inside her chest squeezed.

But before she could work out what it was Matt was propping himself up on his elbows to take his weight and lowering his head to give her a long slow devastating kiss that wiped her mind.

'Like I said,' he murmured, gazing down at her as he gave her a faint smile, 'unbelievable.'

Despite that thing in her chest squeezing even tighter, Laura couldn't help a satisfied smile creeping across her face. Matt gently withdrew from her and rolled onto his back to deal with the condom, then pulled her on top of him and tugged the sheet up over them.

'You know, I've never slept with a king before,' she said, her gaze roaming over the lines of his face.

'I should hope not,' said Matt dryly. 'Most of them are over sixty.'

He trailed his hands over her back and she could feel her skin tingle. She folded her arms on his chest and rested her chin on her wrists. 'How old are you?'

'Thirty-three.'

'Pretty young to become king.'

'I guess.'

'How did it all come about?'

He frowned and the fingers creating havoc on her back stilled. 'Do we have to discuss this now?'

'Why not?'

'Because there are lots of other things we could be doing.'

That was true, she thought, feeling him stirring against her abdomen and beginning to slide beneath the surface of the desire that was sweeping through her. It would be so easy to just give in. Especially with the way Matt's hands had moved lower and were now stroking her bottom and sending tingles all the way round to her core.

But she wanted to know about him. Had done for weeks, and to absolutely no avail. Matt was as chatty as a clam. Torquemada himself would have trouble getting Matt to open up, and God knew she was no Torquemada. But now, with him trapped beneath her, all relaxed and amenable and perhaps prepared to lower his guard a fraction, maybe she did have a chance. And who knew, it might be her only opportunity.

Ruthlessly quashing the desire whipping through her, Laura called into service a hitherto dormant will of steel and reached behind her to remove his hands from her bottom. 'Not right now,' she said, placing them either side of his head and keeping them there with hers. 'You know pretty much everything there is to know about me, yet I know virtually nothing about you.'

Matt frowned. That wasn't true, was it? She knew… Hmm. So maybe it was, but that was understandable. He was reserved. And why wouldn't he be, what with journalists constantly hounding him for his life story?

'So read the papers,' he said.

'But I have such a reliable source right here,' she said, looking up at him from beneath her eyelashes and giving him a seductive smile.

If he had any sense whatsoever he'd be levering himself up and heading back to his own room, because Matt didn't do post-coital conversation. Or any conversation of a personal nature, for that matter.

However his body wanted more of her. Much more. He wanted to watch her shatter in his arms again. Wanted to shatter in her arms.

Hmm. Maybe he could dispense with a few facts and then turn his talents to persuading her to find another use for her mouth.

'Fine,' he said. 'My favourite colour is blue.' Cornflower blue, he thought, looking into her eyes and momentarily losing his train of thought. 'My favourite food is chilli and I don't have time for hobbies. Anything else?'

Her eyebrows shot up. 'Are you kidding?' she said softly.

'What do you want to know? Ask me anything.' Whether he'd choose to answer was another matter entirely.

Laura tilted her head on his chest. 'OK,' she said slowly. 'Seeing as you're such a novice at this sort of thing, we'll start with my original question. How did you become king?'

Matt relaxed. That was an easy enough question to answer. 'Six months ago a Sassanian delegate showed up at my office and offered me the job.'

'Just like that?'

'Pretty much.' It hadn't been quite that simple. At first he'd almost summoned security to remove what he'd thought was a madman. But after the delegate had persuaded him to listen, Matt had wasted no time in accepting. His business was well established and so successful that it practically ran itself and, to be honest, he'd been getting a bit restless. The visit from the Sassanian delegate couldn't have come along at a better time.

'Did you know you were heir to the throne?'

'Of course, but my family had been in exile so long we'd more or less forgotten about it.'

'So what happened?'

'They had a coup.'

'Nasty.'

Matt twined his fingers through hers and felt her shiver. 'Actually, not too bad as coups go. It was bloodless. I think the country had come to the end of the road and everyone knew it. It had been in steady decline for years. It was socially, financially and morally bankrupt. Corruption was rife. It still is. Public services are virtually non-existent.'

'And it's down to you to sort it out?'

'Sorting out problems is what I do.'

'Handy.' A smile curved her lips and Matt's stomach tightened.

'Not really,' he said. 'I was told I was the main reason why they voted to restore the monarchy.'

Her eyes widened. 'That sounds pretty drastic. Couldn't they have just employed you as a consultant or something instead?'

'They wouldn't have been able to afford me. This way they get me for free.'

'So cynical.'

'I prefer realistic.' At the look of affront in her eyes on his behalf, something inside him thawed. 'But if it makes you feel better,' he said, faintly bewildered by the feeling, 'I believe they thought a figurehead would unite the country and restore confidence.'

'So no pressure, then.'

'Fortunately I thrive under pressure.'

'What's the plan?'

'I cut out the dead wood and restructure the finances.'

'Sounds simple.'

Matt thought of all the problems he'd already encountered in the short time he'd been here. 'It isn't.'

'How's it going?'

'Slowly.'

'How does it feel?'

'Feel?'

Laura nodded, watched a frown appear on his forehead and felt him tense. Matt clearly didn't do feelings, at least not of the emotional kind. Well, that was tough, because she was on a roll, and frankly rather stunned by how much he'd divulged, even if it had been all fact based. No way was she giving up now.

'How does what feel?' he muttered.

'The king thing.'

'It doesn't feel anything.'

Matt's expression shuttered but she carried on undeterred.

'It must feel something,' she said cajolingly. 'I don't know, exhilarating, nerve-racking, weighty… Maybe even a little bit scary?'

Matt regarded her thoughtfully, his eyes unfathomable as he appeared to analyse the emotions she'd listed. 'I guess it's challenging,' he said eventually.

Challenging? 'That's it?'

'That's it.'

'Oh.'

'Don't sound so disappointed,' he said, a smile tugging at his mouth. 'You know how much I like challenges.'

'Oh, I do,' said Laura, her eyes darkening and her breathing shallowing for a second before she remembered what she was supposed to be doing and giving herself a quick shake. 'So what have you done with your business?'

'What do you mean?'

'Well, presumably you can't run a business and run a country.'

'I still have it. I've simply taken a step back.'

'Until you decide what you want to do with it?'

'Quite,' he said non-committally.

'And what are you going to do about your house?'

'Which one?'

'How many do you have?'

'A few.'

Naturally. 'I mean the one in Little Somerford.'

'I'm not going to do anything about it.'

'Oh.' She frowned.

'What?'

'Well, I know it's your house and it's really none of my business, but it does seem a shame to leave such a lovely house empty and neglected.'

She felt his heart thump. 'It's not neglected. A gardener goes in twice a week and I employ a part-time caretaker.'

'OK,' said Laura, nibbling on her lip and ignoring the feeling she might be treading on eggshells. 'Maybe neglected isn't quite the right word. Unloved would be better.'

'Unloved?' He frowned. 'It's a house. It doesn't need to be loved.'

She gasped and gave him a quick smile. 'Wash your mouth out. All buildings deserve to be loved. How long have you had it?'

'Eight years.'

'And how much time have you spent there?'

'Not a lot.'

'That would explain the emotional neglect.'

His expression tightened. 'I'm busy.'

'That's no excuse.' Laura sniffed. 'I bet you wouldn't let one of your businesses slide into neglect.'

'True. But then I'm not looking to make a profit on the house.'

'Just as well. You know,' she mused, 'if I owned something like that I wouldn't be able to stay away.'

'Unfortunately I don't have that luxury,' he murmured, his gaze dropping to her mouth.

'It breaks my heart to see something like that drifting into decline. If you're not going to maintain it, and if you're hardly ever there, what's the point of having it?'

Matt lifted his gaze. 'I like having it.'

Her eyes widened. 'It's a status symbol?'

His eyes went bleak and Laura's heart squeezed. 'If you like,' he said.

'Oh, the poor thing,' she murmured. 'No wonder it was so lonely.'

'Lonely?' His tone suggested he thought she was nuts.

'Yes, lonely. A house like that should be alive. Filled with laughter and activity and a family. There should be hordes of children running all over the place.'

He tensed and she sensed barriers springing up all around him. 'Perhaps.'

'Do you have any family?'

'Not much. I'm an only child. My father died of cancer when I was sixteen. My mother lives in London.'

'Don't *you* get lonely?'

He froze beneath her. 'No,' he said gruffly. 'I'm better off alone.'

Her chest tightened at the bleak look that haunted his eyes. 'That's sad,' she said softly.

And then he rolled over, trapping her beneath him and Laura's heart began to thump and her breath began to quicken. 'So make it better,' he muttered, lowering his head and covering her mouth with his.

Matt watched Laura sleeping. Stared at the fingers of moonlight turning her blond hair to silver and listened as her breath whispered across his chest.

And with every rise of her breasts, every fall, every soft breath he felt another tiny strand of his carefully controlled life unravel.

Dammit, how could he have been so careless? What was it about Laura that had him lowering his guard and revealing so much about himself like that?

He didn't do feelings. Hadn't done for years. He didn't need her making him question decisions he'd made years ago. So why was he?

Why did she have him suddenly doubting his role on Sassania? His belief he was better off alone? And what was all that nonsense about his house needing to be loved?

Matt's heart hardened and he told himself not to be so absurd. His role on Sassania was clear. He liked being alone. And just because he hadn't ever got round to sorting out the house he'd bought intending to live in it with a wife and family, it didn't mean anything.

Laura and her pseudo-psychiatry could take a hike. He really didn't need it. He was fine the way he was.

So why did he find himself wanting to tell her *more*?

Matt's heart thudded and his blood ran cold. Feeling highly unsettled, he eased himself from beneath her arm, swung his legs over the bed and got up. He pulled on his clothes and ran his hands through his hair.

Staring down at her as her mouth twitched in her sleep, he fought the urge to throw his clothes off and get back into bed with her, and picked up his shoes.

That kind of thinking led to madness.

He needed time to regroup. Regain some sort of control and decide what the hell to do about everything.

Work was the solution, he thought, heading to the door and sanity. Work was *always* the solution. And as neither Laura nor the attraction he seemed to have to her showed any signs of going away, maybe it wouldn't be a bad idea to put some physical distance between them.

There was bound to be a conference going on about something somewhere in the world.

Laura felt sunshine prick her eyes, gingerly opened them and then grinned and stretched.

Wow. What a night. Every muscle in her body ached with a delicious kind of languor. In between acquainting herself with every inch of him and vice versa she'd lost count of the number of orgasms she'd had.

But the spectacular sex aside, what was giving her an even warmer glow this morning was the fact that Matt had opened up. Just a crack, but far more than she'd thought he would have done.

OK, so she'd asked the questions, and he hadn't volunteered much that she hadn't asked, but to be honest she hadn't expected him to venture anything at all. But he had and the balance in their relationship was definitely moving in her direction. Which was progress.

Laura froze mid-stretch and her heart lurched. Hang on a second? Progress? What was that all about? Since when had progress mattered? And since when did she and Matt have a relationship? The last thing she wanted was a relationship. She and Matt weren't about relationships and progress, were they? No. They were just about sex. With any luck lots of it.

In fact she might just remind him of that very thing right now.

Fizzing all over with desire, Laura rolled over, fully expecting to slam up against the hard warm naked body of Matt, but instead met nothing but cool air.

Oh. Desire vanished as she sat up and felt the pillow that still bore the indentation of his head. Cold. Hmm. So much for embarking on a raging affair right now. Matt's absence did not bode well for a long leisurely start to the day.

Nor did the note she suddenly spied on the bedside table. Clutching the sheet and wrapping it beneath her arms, she rolled over, picked it up and then fell back against the pillows.

Gone to Athens. Didn't want to wake you.

Laura read the note twice. Not that she needed to when the message was perfectly clear, but the first time she'd got a bit distracted admiring his handwriting and remembering the feel of his hands on her body.

But when she read it a second time the bottom fell out of her stomach and disappointment flooded through her.

Gone to Athens? Laura didn't know what to think.

Matt hadn't mentioned anything about a trip so what on earth was he doing in Athens? Especially when they'd scheduled a meeting for this afternoon to discuss the budget for the restoration work.

And why hadn't he wanted to wake her? She wouldn't have minded. Surely he hadn't had to leave so suddenly there hadn't been time for a quick goodbye. Surely she was worth more than eight words, one apostrophe and two full stops.

And after what they'd shared she deserved a kiss at the very least.

Laura's throat tightened as the note slipped from her fingers and fluttered to the bed. That wasn't fair. She wasn't forgettable. She wasn't dispensable. And she wasn't going to have another man walk all over her.

CHAPTER TEN

SO MUCH for assuming that out of sight out of mind might actually work, thought Matt grimly, striding along the corridor to his suite and scowling. Attending the conference in Athens had been a complete waste of time in that respect.

From a professional point of view it couldn't have gone better. He'd networked, held discussions and drawn up agreements.

People had congratulated him on his new role and he'd been able to answer their questions about his plans for the country, for the first time feeling confident that he knew what he was talking about.

But while all that had been going on he hadn't been able to get Laura out of his head and it was driving him demented. Much more of this tension and this aching, this clawing kind of need, and he'd snap. He'd start making mistakes and the Sassanians would wonder what the hell they'd done in voting in favour of him to restore their battered country.

Maybe he should just give in and suggest a fling. A fling didn't mean a relationship, did it? A fling just meant lots of the mind-blowing sex he'd been missing and very little conversation.

Matt stalked into his dressing room, yanking his tie

off and undoing the top button of his shirt. He flung his jacket over the back of a chair and kicked off his shoes. A cold shower. That was what he needed. And then he'd seek her out, put his proposal to her and see what she had to say.

He undid the buttons of his shirt, tugged it from his trousers and marched through to his bedroom.

And stopped dead.

Laura was standing by the French doors that opened onto his private terrace, the sun streaming in behind her giving her a blazing kind of corona.

For a second Matt thought he was hallucinating. That somehow his feverish imagination was playing tricks on him.

But then she jumped, her gazed dipped to his bare chest and she let out a little gasp and from the heat that suddenly whipped through him Matt realised she was no hallucination.

Which, on reflection, was great. He was so hard it hurt. Whatever the reason she was in his bedroom, her timing couldn't be more perfect.

'Good trip?' she said, the ice in her voice slamming a brake on his thoughts.

Hmm. Matt went still. Perhaps suggesting a fling at right this moment might not be wise. With the hostility rolling off her in his direction, he'd probably get a slap in the face.

'Great,' he said, wondering why she was quite so frosty.

'I'm so glad.'

'What are you doing in my bedroom?'

'Waiting for you. I heard you were back.'

'I was just about to take a shower,' he said, taking his shirt off and seeing her little white teeth catch her lip.

'Why did you leave without saying goodbye?'

That was what the hostility was about? Matt rubbed his jaw. He'd left without saying goodbye because he hadn't been able to trust himself not to get all caught up again in the spell she'd woven over him. He'd done it for all the right reasons, but that didn't stop the trace of hurt in her voice making a stab of guilt dart through him.

'Didn't you get my note?'

'I did.'

Matt shoved the guilt aside. 'That explained everything.'

'Eight words, Matt. Eight words. After the night we shared do you really think they explained everything?'

Well, yes, he did. He couldn't have put it more simply. 'I didn't want to wake you.'

'I wouldn't have minded.'

But he would have.

'You want to know what I think?' she said, tilting her head and shooting him a shrewd glance.

Not really. He had no intention of discussing his motives for hurtling off to Athens. 'What?' he said, because she was probably going to tell him anyway.

'I think you were avoiding me.'

The air in the room thickened. Grew warmer. Tighter. Matt's eyes narrowed. How had she managed to work that out? 'Nonsense,' he said flatly.

'Is it?'

'Why would I be avoiding you?'

'That's what I haven't been able to work out.'

Matt shrugged. 'There's nothing to work out. The opportunity to attend the conference in Athens to discuss alternative sources of energy simply cropped up at the last minute, that's all.'

'That's what Antonio said. Very last minute apparently.'

'It was important.'

'More important than our meeting to discuss the cost of the work I'm doing?'

Ah. Matt went still. He was caught between a rock and a hard place. If he agreed, he'd upset her, and that wouldn't be conducive to persuading her to have a fling, but if he denied it then she'd really wonder why he'd gone.

'You're right,' he said, deciding that focusing on her earlier concerns was his only way out. It had the added benefit of appeasing his conscience. 'I should have said goodbye. I'm sorry I didn't.'

Laura frowned. 'Waking up alone didn't feel nice. It made everything we'd done seem a bit sordid.'

God. Sordid was the last thing it had been. 'I'm sorry,' he said again. 'Anything I can do to remedy the situation just let me know.'

Laura nodded and bit her lip. 'There is something you could do.'

'What?'

She tilted her head and gave him a slow smile that had relief spinning through him and his heart hammering. 'Give me my goodbye kiss now.'

Matt's body tightened with anticipation and lust. 'I could do that. But I should warn you that it probably wouldn't stop there.'

Her eyes took on a sparkle that he felt in the pit of his stomach. 'I was kind of counting on it.'

'What were you thinking of?' He knew what he was thinking of.

'Sex. Illicit sex. And lots of it. Without any strings attached whatsoever.'

Matt's pulse began to thunder. 'Are you sure?' She really didn't seem the type.

'I've never been surer of anything. With my relationship history I don't want strings and I don't want complications. A relationship is the last thing on the planet I need right now. I find them stifling and suffocating and I feel like I've just started to learn how to breathe. So all I want from you is multiple orgasms. What do you think?'

What did he think? His head was so fuzzy he could barely think at all. Because, God, she really was perfect. 'I think it's an excellent idea,' he said hoarsely.

'Good.' She gave him a sexy little smile that had lust pounding through him. 'So about that shower you mentioned…'

It was a good thing Laura hadn't been planning to finish that sentence because as Matt suddenly sprang forwards and scooped her up in his arms her breath whooshed from her lungs and lust robbed her of the power of speech.

She'd taken such a gamble. Offering herself to him for nothing more than a fling like that. It was so reckless. So uncharacteristic. But she was sick of being sensible. She'd been there, done that, and had still ended up dumped and jobless and miserable.

And what was so awful about a fling anyway? She'd spent the entire week that Matt had been away thinking about it. Weighing up the pros and cons and driving herself to distraction with her endless analysis.

In the end she'd thought what the hell? A fling was

temporary. A fling was hot. Best of all a fling was not a relationship.

And now, thank God, it looked as if her gamble was about to pay off. In spades.

Wrapping her arms around Matt's neck, she clung on for dear life as he carried her across the room to the bathroom. His heart hammered against her shoulder. She could feel his muscles taut and tense and rippling with the effort of carrying her. Gazed at all that bare brown skin in such close proximity and couldn't resist planting a hot wet kiss to the pulse pounding at the base of his neck.

Matt swore softly and his arms tightened around her. A shudder ripped through her. She felt an answering one run through him. So she did it again.

He shoved a shoulder against the bathroom door and lowered her to her feet. Clamped one arm around her waist to keep her against him, and reached out with the other to switch on the shower.

Bringing his mouth down on hers, he unzipped her dress, slid the straps down her arms and it fell in a pool at her feet. Laura kicked it aside and grappled with his trousers. Matt unclipped her bra and it fell to the floor. And then off came knickers and shorts and he was backing her into the shower.

Laura gasped as needles of water hammered down over her, making her already highly sensitised skin tingle and fizzle even more. And then his mouth was on hers again and his hands were sliding over her back, up and down her sides and over her breasts.

He reached for the soap but she took it from him and gave him a tiny smile.

'Let me. All that travelling must have been quite exhausting.'

'It wasn't the travelling.'

'You didn't really go all the way to Athens just to discuss alternative sources of energy, did you?'

'No.'

Hah. She'd been so right. He *had* been avoiding her.

A flicker of amusement flared in his eyes. 'I also discussed the possibility of raising finance via the issuance of government bonds.'

'Oh.'

'And if this is what I can expect on my return I must do it more often.'

If that was what he wanted to pretend, she was fine with that. Laura grinned. 'Turn around.'

The flicker of amusement faded. 'Only a fool would turn his back on such a dangerous smile.'

'I'm only armed with shower gel. I'm hardly dangerous.'

'You think?' he murmured.

A tiny crease appeared between his brows and she lifted a hand to smooth it away. 'I promise I'll be gentle. Turn around.'

Matt's eyes glittered but he did as she asked and planted his hands high on the wall.

Faced with the sexiest back view she'd ever seen, Laura swallowed. She squeezed a ball of gel into her palms and then pressed her hands to his shoulders. Rubbing and squeezing and pressing, she massaged her way over his shoulders, down his back. Touching and exploring every inch of him, every dip, every contour.

She felt his skin tighten, felt his muscles clench as her hands moved over his body. The water cascaded down him, sending the suds rippling to the floor. As inch after inch of glorious back was revealed, Laura put her hands on his arms and moved forwards so that her mouth could follow the same trail as her hands had just made.

Her breasts brushed against his back. She heard his sharp intake of breath, felt him brace himself. As desire began to whip through her Laura slid her hands down his sides, curved one round his waist and wrapped her fingers around the hard length of his erection.

His penis leapt beneath her touch, and as she started to move her hand along the length of him he let out a low groan. His great body shook as she explored him. She felt him shudder, heard his breathing roughen.

Removing her hand, she stood up on her tiptoes and whispered in his ear, 'Turn around.'

'If I do, I might not be responsible for the consequences.'

'I'll take full responsibility,' she said huskily, moving back a little, giving him room to turn.

And then she gave him no room at all. Pushing him up against the glass wall, she began to kiss her way down his body. His skin twitched beneath her lips and when she knelt and took him in her mouth, he groaned.

'God, Laura,' he said roughly as she ran her hands over his thighs.

His hands dug into her hair and she felt him shudder as she took him deeper. She heard him moan, curse softly, could sense the battle raging within him as he clung on to control.

She wanted him to lose it. She wanted him as desperate for her as she was for him. But then he was pulling her head back and hauling her to her feet and gathering her into his arms. 'Enough,' he muttered, his eyes blazing into hers and making the desire swirling around inside her grow and spread and burn.

'Not nearly,' Laura said, winding her arms around his

neck and kissing him fiercely as he switched the water off and lifted her into his arms.

But when *would* be enough?

The thought hammered in Matt's head as he strode to the bed with Laura curled in his arms. Because right now, with desire coursing through him, his head pounding and his entire body aching with need, he didn't think he'd ever get enough of her.

He lowered her onto the sheets and stared down at her for a second. Her lips were red and swollen from their kiss. Her eyes shone and the smile she was giving him made something in the region of his chest squeeze.

The blood rushing through his head, Matt sank onto the bed beside her. But as he rolled on top of her Laura wound her leg around his and rolled them over again so that she was on top of him.

'Forget the travelling,' she said, giving him a demure little smile that made his stomach clench. 'Carrying me all over the place must be utterly draining.'

'You don't weigh much.'

She shrugged. 'Indulge me. I've had plenty of opportunity to Embrace Confrontation and say no. But I think my "getting what I want" needs more work and right now I want you to just lie back and let me have my wicked way with you.'

Desire hammered through him. 'Oh. Well, in that case, it would be churlish of me to interfere with your journey to self-discovery.'

'Precisely.'

'In fact you can practise on me all you like.'

'You're too kind,' she said, lowering her head and brushing her lips against his. So tantalisingly brief Matt's heart practically stopped.

'Not kind,' he muttered. 'Totally selfish.'

Then she angled her head, set her lips to his and slipped her tongue into his mouth and his blood began to boil. Matt tangled his hand into her wet hair and swept the other down her back over her bottom to pull her tightly against him.

She went still for a second, moaned and then began to move. He felt himself growing harder against her. So hard he was hurting. Matt winced at the ferocity of the ache that gripped him.

'Are you all right?' Laura breathed against his mouth.

'I'm not entirely sure.'

'Where do you hurt?'

'Why?' What was she going to do? Torment him further?

'Maybe I can kiss you better.' Oh, yes, definitely torment him further.

'For God's sake, Laura,' he muttered. 'I'm not made of stone.'

'So I can tell.'

He gripped her head and kissed her so long, so thoroughly and so hard he couldn't think straight.

'Condoms,' she gasped.

Thank God someone was still faintly in possession of their faculties. 'In the drawer.'

She leaned away from him, fumbled for a second, then rolled one over him. Nearly passing out with the effort of not climaxing right then and there, Matt gritted his teeth and lifted her onto him.

Laura moaned and bit her lip and Matt's hands curled into fists with the strain of letting her take charge. She closed her eyes and rotated her hips and panted. Matt's head swam. His penis throbbed deep inside her. His heart thundered and as her pants became quicker, shorter, more and more ragged, her movements jerkier and more out of control, he couldn't stand it any longer.

Rearing up, he clasped her against him and flipped her over. Swallowing her gasp of shock he anchored her legs around his waist and mindlessly drove into her.

Shock flashed in her eyes and then vanished as they glazed over with passion. Laura's nails raked his back as he kissed her. She clutched at his shoulders. Threw her head back and groaned. He swallowed her whimpers and broke off the kiss to explore the soft skin of her neck with his mouth.

Clinging on to his control by his fingertips and on the point of losing his mind, Matt pulled out of her and then thrust again, utterly unable to stop himself from burying himself as deep inside her as he could.

And then he heard her cry out his name as shudders racked her body. She convulsed around him, drawing him in deeper and tighter. With that last remnant of control spiralling off, Matt drove into her once more and hurtled into oblivion.

It took several minutes for his heart to slow and his breathing to steady. When they did, it was as if the whole room had been tossed in the air and had settled differently. Almost the same but not quite.

A smugly satisfied smile curved her lips and his pulse began to speed up all over again. 'Oh, I *knew* this was a good idea.'

Matt wasn't so sure. Something suddenly made him think an affair with Laura was a very bad idea. However no-strings.

'You,' she said, fluttering her eyelashes up at him, 'are incredible.'

So was she. Pretty irresistible, too. And a dozen other things he really didn't want to think about.

'I really do have to go,' he said, leaning away from her, picking up his watch off the floor and frowning.

'Now?'

'Yes.'

'Oh. Well. Of course,' she said lightly, pulling the sheet up over her chest and tucking it beneath her arms. 'Maybe we could have lunch?'

Matt shook his head and got up. 'I have a meeting.' Lunch, or any kind of interaction that wasn't of the horizontal and naked sort for that matter, wasn't an option.

Her face fell and a flash of disappointment flickered in her eyes. 'Sure,' she said, with a smile that he thought looked a little forced. 'Fine. I guess I'll see you around, then.'

That wasn't what he'd meant, either. Feeling like a heel, Matt leaned down and gave her a long slow kiss. 'What are you doing tonight?' he said, pulling back before he could decide to cancel his meeting and spend the rest of the afternoon in bed with Laura.

'Nothing.' A relieved grin spread across her face and his heart suddenly thumped with something that felt weirdly like alarm.

'I'll see you later,' he muttered, telling himself not to be ridiculous. A casual affair with Laura was nothing to get alarmed about.

'Great.'

Except it wasn't all that great, thought Laura, sitting in the library and idly flipping through a book of old photographs and plans a fortnight later.

At first she'd been only too happy with the arrangement. It had been her idea after all, and as they'd seen each other every night since Matt had returned from

Athens she didn't really have anything to complain about. Her horizons had been broadened considerably and the sex had been getting better and better. And as a bonus, her body, having never been put to such energetic use, was more toned than ever before.

Her fling with Matt was exactly what she'd wanted. Hot hassle-free fun.

So why was it leaving her feeling increasingly dissatisfied?

Laura closed the book with a thump, sat back and frowned. Why did it hurt that he didn't ever seem to want to meet up for lunch? Or dinner, or on any of the other occasions she'd suggested? Why did it hurt that he never asked her to do anything other than spread herself across the nearest available flat surface?

When had hot casual sex become not enough?

Suddenly finding the library stifling, Laura got up and stepped out onto the terrace. The breeze caressed her skin as she wandered across the stone, leaned her elbows on the balustrade and gazed over the gardens.

Oh, God. Maybe, despite all her efforts to convince herself otherwise, she just wasn't cut out for an affair. Maybe Kate had been right, and she was more of a commitment fiend than she'd realised.

And if that *was* the case, she thought, following the path of a butterfly as it fluttered from one exotic flower to another, where did it leave her? Her mind whirred. Did that mean she *did* actually want a relationship? With Matt?

Her heart sank. God, she hoped not. Because what a disaster that would be. She could still recall the look on Matt's face when she'd suggested their fling. His relief when she'd told him she wanted nothing more from him than mind-blowing orgasms couldn't have been more transparent.

Wanting a relationship with Matt would bring nothing but pain and she'd be an idiot to hope for more than a fling.

But the more she thought about it, the more undeniable it became. And the more undeniable it became, the faster her heart plummeted.

Uh-oh.

Who'd she been trying to fool?

She *did* want more than just mind-blowing sex. She wanted to know what Matt was thinking. What he was feeling. All the time. She wanted to know what had made him the man he'd become and what his dreams were. She wanted to know how he felt about the death of his father and why he was so driven. She wanted to share her life, her dreams with him.

She wanted everything.

Which so hadn't been part of the deal.

Laura pinched the bridge of her nose and sighed. Matt would never agree to accommodate her on any of that. That night he'd spilled out all the stuff about himself had been a blip. One he clearly regretted making, judging by the way he'd vanished to the other side of Europe at first light.

Ever since then, he'd revealed absolutely nothing. And neither had she. The last thing he'd want would be her poking and prodding at his psyche.

Unless, of course, he'd been thinking the same…

No. Laura straightened and planted her hands on the balustrade. That was nuts. Nothing more than extremely wishful thinking on her part. Because she was pretty sure that Matt was *not* sitting at his desk right this second wanting to share his dreams with her and figuring out what she wanted.

That kind of thinking could only lead to heartache.

But it didn't stop her mind racing. Wondering if he *might*. Wondering what would happen if he did.

Her heart pounding, Laura set her jaw. Whatever Matt's frame of mind, whatever he might or might not be thinking, a casual fling was no longer what she wanted and she couldn't carry on pretending it was.

So she therefore had two possible courses of action. She could either take the cowardly way out and board the next plane home or she could pluck up her courage, risk everything, and ask him.

CHAPTER ELEVEN

'SO HOW was your day?'

Matt lay back and felt a warm kind of satisfaction steal over him. His day had been tougher than most. He'd had to authorise the arrest of a number of government officials and there was a problem with the funding of the new hospital. The only thing that had kept him going had been the thought of losing himself in the soft warmth of Laura's body. And it had been every bit as amazing as he'd expected.

'Fine,' he said, rubbing his eyes and tucking her in closer.

'Surely it can't be fine every day.'

Matt sighed as a wave of fatigue washed over him. 'What do you want me to say, Laura?' he murmured against her hair. 'Do you really want to spend the time we have together discussing the intricacies of Sassanian politics?'

She wriggled away from him and propped herself up on her elbow. 'Well, why not?'

'Because, frankly, I have enough of that during the day.'

'Then maybe we could talk about something else.'

'Why do we have to talk at all?'

'Because we never talk,' she said calmly, 'and I don't think it's natural.'

We never talk. All you do is work.

Despite the lingering heat still flickering through his body, Matt's blood ran cold as echoes of Alicia's hurt-filled accusations reverberated around his head. And just like eight years ago, his brain switched into neutral and his body filled with the familiar hammering instinct to escape.

'I don't have time for this,' he muttered, throwing back the sheet, getting out of bed and reaching for his jeans.

But Laura got there first, yanked them from him and snatched them out of reach. 'Now who's running away?'

Matt froze. He wasn't running away. Was he? Still? Realisation slapped him in the face. God, he was. Look at the way he'd gone to Athens just because Laura had managed to wangle a few snippets of information out of him. And now look how desperate he was to dash back to his suite just because she wanted to talk.

And what was so dangerous about talking anyway? People did it all the time.

'Fine,' he said, pulling on what few clothes still remained within his grasp and lying back on the bed. 'What do you want to talk about?'

He heard her take a deep breath and all the hairs on his body quivered in alarm. 'Us.'

Matt frowned. 'What about us?' As far as he was concerned there wasn't an 'us'.

'Where do you see this going?'

'Why does it have to be going anywhere?'

There was a long silence. 'I'll take that as a "nowhere", then, shall I?'

'What's wrong with carrying on the way we are?'

'Aren't you getting bored?'

'No.' And then a horrible thought struck him. Maybe *she'd* had enough. 'Are you?' As the possibility that she might say yes flashed into his head something in the region of his chest began to ache.

'Not exactly.'

The force of the relief that lurched through him nearly winded him. 'What does that mean?'

'Well, the sex is fine—'

'Fine?'

A tiny smile flashed across her face. 'OK, much better than fine.' The smile faded and his stomach clenched. 'But it's all we ever do.'

'What's wrong with that? I thought that was what we agreed. What you wanted?'

Laura let out a sigh. 'It was. I did.'

'But?' He turned his head to look at her, and then when her eyes met his and he saw what was in them wished he hadn't.

'I want more.'

In the silence that followed Matt's heart plummeted. He should have known a no-strings affair with Laura was too good to be true. For, despite all her protests to the contrary, hadn't he had the niggling suspicion that she was no more cut out for a casual fling than he was for a full-blown relationship? Yes, he had. She was a relationship kind of girl.

But had he listened? No. Because it had been easier not to. And now he was suffering the consequences of his one moment of weakness.

He had to put the record straight. In no uncertain terms, because the tiny flame of hope flickering in her eyes was making his stomach churn. He wasn't about to casually knock down eight years of carefully built up barriers of self-preservation. For anyone.

'I thought you weren't interested in more,' he said flatly.

'So did I.' Laura lifted her shoulders. 'I was wrong.'

'Well, I can't give you more.'

At the rigidity of his expression and the bleakness of his tone Laura's heart wrenched. Oh, God. She should have taken the first course of action and simply got on the first plane out of here. Because this conversation wasn't looking good. In fact she was pretty sure that continuing it would only end in pain. Her pain. Yet she wanted to know why he was unable to give her more. Badly. 'Can't or won't?'

Matt's jaw clenched. 'Either.'

'Why not?'

'It wouldn't be fair on the Sassanians.'

Laura blinked. 'What on earth do they have to do with anything?'

'If I got into a relationship there'd be talk of queens and heirs and I won't let them get all excited about that when I'm not planning to stay.'

What? *That* was his excuse for his emotional obstinacy? Gossip? She'd never heard anything so ridiculous in her life. And then the last few words sank in and Laura fought not to gape. 'You're not planning to stay?'

'No,' he muttered, suddenly scowling as if furious he'd let that slip. Well, that was tough. Curiosity spun through her, briefly nudging the need to find out why he was so reluctant to commit to one side.

'Why?' she asked.

'I have a global business. My general manager can't run it for ever. I need to get back to it at some point.'

'But what about Sassania? And the Sassanians?'

'It'll be fine. They'll be fine.' A muscle began to hammer in his jaw. 'I'll leave it in the best state possible. I'm very good at what I do.'

'I don't doubt it. But this is a country. Not a business.'

'Same principles. CEO… King… They're just titles.'

Laura frowned. 'Surely it's more than that.'

'Not really.'

'But what about the people? Don't you feel some sort of duty towards them? Some sort of loyalty?'

Matt stiffened. 'I'm here to do a job. Nothing more, nothing less.'

'It's just a job?'

Matt glowered at her. 'What else would it be? A hundred years ago, the Sassanians executed my great-great-grandfather and sent my family into exile. I've never been here. Why would I have any sense of loyalty?'

Laura blinked. 'Well, I suppose I don't really know. I just assumed you would. Why else would you put such a lot of effort into the role?'

'I'm a perfectionist. Sassania has a smaller population than the workforce of some of the companies I've worked with, and an infinitely smaller budget. It's no big deal. Once the country's back on its feet the people can decide how they want to continue and who they want to take over.'

'And they know this is your vision, do they?'

'I've made no secret of the fact that I intend to return to my company. I've spent years building it up. Years of hard work and sacrifice. I'm not just going to give it all up because of some ancestral thing I had no influence over.'

'Well, I think that's awful.'

Matt's jaw tightened. 'I don't care what you think and I don't need to have my decisions questioned.'

'Well, you should.'

Matt's eyebrows shot up. 'What?'

'You're good at the king thing. I've heard people talking about you. They have high hopes of you and like it or not if you leave you'll be letting them down and leaving them far worse off than any dictator. And you know, you say you don't care about duty and loyalty and the people of this country, but you do. Why else would you have spent so much time working for it over the past fortnight?'

'To avoid precisely this kind of conversation,' Matt snapped.

Laura felt as if someone had thumped her in the solar plexus. Her breath shot from her lungs and her head went fuzzy.

He'd immersed himself in his work specifically so he wouldn't have to spend time getting to know her? Something inside her began to shake. Did he *really* think all she was good for was evening entertainment?

Oh, God. How could she have got it so wrong? Hadn't she secretly been hoping that that wishful thinking wouldn't be quite so wishful? That he'd listen to her and give her that thoughtful little look he often gave her when he was tossing something around in his head, and agree? That he'd lean over, tell her she was right, give her a long slow kiss and suggest they give it a shot?

Laura's heart began to ache. She was such an idiot. Would she never learn? 'Oh,' she said eventually. 'I see.'

Matt frowned. 'Have I ever given you the impression I was interested in anything else?'

'No.' He hadn't. She'd got it wrong all on her own.

Complete and utter fool. Why had she ever embarked on this conversation? Why couldn't she have stayed happy to carry on until their fling ended? Why had she ever been on that assertiveness course?

'So why can't you give me anything more?'

And why was she such a masochist?

Matt rubbed a hand over his face and pinched the bridge of his nose. 'I just can't.'

He vibrated with tension and Laura suddenly felt as if she were skating on very thin ice miles from the safety of the shore. But she had to know.

'That is not an answer to the question, Matt. If you really think you're leaving,' she said, thinking about the excuse he'd given her, 'you're deluding yourself.'

'Frankly, I don't really care what you think.'

Oh, that hurt. The pain that scythed through her nearly made her pass out. 'You bastard,' she breathed.

Matt flinched as if she'd struck him. 'OK, fine,' he bit out, his eyes suddenly blazing. 'You want to know the real reason why I don't want a relationship? Because relationships are messy,' he snapped. 'They sap your energy, your time and they screw up your judgement.'

The bitterness in his voice cut right through her and her heart clenched at the bleakness of his face. 'What happened?'

'I don't want to talk about it.'

'I know you don't. But you're going to have to, because I'm channelling Module Three, and without your jeans you can't escape.'

The ghost of a smile flickered at his mouth and then vanished. Matt rubbed his hand over his face and let out a heavy sigh. 'The last relationship I had was with my then fiancée, and it didn't end well.'

In the silence that followed his words you could have heard a pin drop.

Matt had been engaged?

Laura's brain began to pound. To whom? When? How? And what had gone wrong? God, there was so much she didn't know about this man.

'You were engaged?' she said faintly.

'I was.'

'When?'

'Eight years ago.'

'What happened?'

Matt shrugged as if he couldn't care less, but his face was tight and a tiny flicker of turmoil flashed in the depths of his eyes. 'Nothing spectacular. We were young. We simply drifted apart and eventually split up.'

'If it was nothing spectacular then why haven't you had a relationship since?'

'I haven't had the time.'

She didn't believe that for a second. 'What was her name?'

'Alicia.'

'Did you love her?'

'I asked her to marry me.'

'Not quite what I asked.'

His eyes flashed. 'Yes, I did.'

Laura ignored the stab of jealousy that struck her chest. 'So what went wrong?'

'Do you ever give up?'

Laura gave him a tiny smile. 'Not any longer.'

'My work got in the way.' Ah. 'The business was at a fragile stage. On the point of taking off. I had to devote a lot of time to it.'

'And Alicia didn't appreciate that?'

'Not particularly. Apparently we stopped communicating. *I* stopped communicating.'

'Fancy that,' murmured Laura.

'The less we communicated, the more we argued. The end was inevitable.'

'Does it still hurt?'

His jaw tightened. 'No.'

'So why still be so against relationships? They don't all fail.'

'I'm well aware of that,' he said tightly.

Laura took a deep breath and put her life in Matt's hands. 'So why don't we do this properly?'

'Do what?'

'You and me.'

'No.'

'Why not?'

'I still don't have the time.'

'That's such a cop out.'

'What?'

'Well, it is. You could make time. You know what? I think that deep down you're scared.'

'Rubbish.'

'Is it? I think you're scared that if you allow yourself to try a real relationship it'll hurt.'

'If that's what you want to think, be my guest.'

Why was he being so stubborn about this? Would she ever get through to him? Would he ever give them a chance?

And why did it matter so much that he did?

The inescapable truth smacked her in the face and her heart stopped. And then began to thunder.

Her head went fuzzy and a cold sweat broke out over her entire body.

God. No. That was impossible. She couldn't be…

She thought about the way up until now he'd made her feel. The giddy anticipation with which she'd looked forward to their nights together. The admiration and respect she had for the work he was doing, for the man he was.

She thought about the idea of leaving, of never seeing Matt ever again, or never being able to touch him again, and agony unlike any she'd ever known cut through her.

She was…

She was in love with Matt. She was head over heels in love with a man who was only interested in a fling.

And there wasn't a thing she could do about it.

Laura began to shake as anguish gripped every cell of her body. 'I think I should leave.'

Matt frowned. 'You don't have to leave.'

'Oh, I do.' Even though she longed to stay.

'Why?'

'You don't have a monopoly on self-preservation, Matt,' she said, giving him a shaky smile. 'We want different things, and that's never going to change, is it?'

His face was blank and it broke her heart. 'No. Fine. Go.'

'I'll send over a list of people I'd recommend to continue the restoration work.'

'Fine.'

'Is that all you can say?'

Matt shoved his hands through his hair. 'What else is there?'

So it was over. It shouldn't hurt so much. But the pain… The excruciating pain… Laura got to her feet and her legs nearly gave way. Somehow she managed to stand. Somehow she pulled on her clothes, but her fingers felt too thick and were shaking too much to do up her buttons.

'I know you think you're better off alone, Matt,' she said, pulling her shirt tightly around her as if that could somehow stop the cold seeping through her, 'but you aren't. No one is. Work won't keep you warm at night. Work won't be there for you when you have a bad day or when you're old and grey. I would.'

Matt shrugged and she wanted to shake him. Thump him. Make him hurt as much as he was making her hurt. Because he must know how she felt about him.

'I never wanted it to end like this, Laura,' he said flatly.

Laura's heart cracked wide open and a wretchedness more devastating than she'd ever known spun through her. 'Neither did I.'

CHAPTER TWELVE

THAT things with Laura had ended was for the best, Matt told himself for the hundredth time in the week since she'd left.

He didn't miss her prodding at his psyche or her incessant questioning one little bit. Nor did he miss the way those eyes of hers looked at him and seemed to drill right into his soul. And he certainly didn't miss her. He missed the sex, that was all. Which was absolutely fine because he would get over that eventually.

No. He was glad she'd gone. Thrilled in fact. He couldn't be happier. The conversation they'd had the night before she'd left had cemented in his mind exactly why he didn't do relationships and he'd been right to let her leave.

So why was he feeling so out of sorts? Why did he feel as if he were wading through treacle simply to get through the days? Why couldn't he focus? And why wasn't this run that he was in the middle of doing anything to relieve the tension in his body?

Undoubtedly it was the abrupt way their fling had ended, Matt decided, his feet thumping along the path that circled the lake. She'd ended it before he'd been ready to let her go, and that irritated him beyond belief. He should have been more persuasive in making her stay. He should have knocked that conversation on the head and simply made love to her until she was too breathless to talk.

If he'd had any sense at all, he thought, his lungs pumping hard enough to burst, he would have avoided getting involved with her in the first place. That would have saved him a whole lot of trouble.

But never mind.

Sooner or later he'd regain the ability to sleep at night.

Sooner or later he'd fall back into the swing of getting Sassania back on its feet.

And sooner or later he'd find someone to take on the work of restoring the country's monuments. So what if none of the people she'd recommended had been quite right?

It was simply a question of time, that was all.

But what if he didn't?

The thought slammed into his head and Matt stumbled. What if he never stopped tossing and turning and dreaming of her? What if he never got his focus back? What if she was irreplaceable?

No. That was absurd. He would. He had to. And no one was irreplaceable. Especially not someone who'd been so wrong about everything.

Or had she?

Matt's head went so fuzzy he thought he might be about to pass out. He stopped. Bent over and planted his hands on this thighs, his heart pounding and breath ragged.

Oh, God. She hadn't been wrong. The realisation banged around his head, making his body feel far weaker than the run had.

He *did* want to stay on the island and he *was* sick of always being alone.

And if she'd been right about that then what else had she been right about? *Was* he scared? No, he wasn't scared of anything.

Except possibly the depth of his feelings for Laura.

Matt froze and he shot up, his knees nearly buckling. His head throbbed. Spun. The barriers he'd built up around his heart suddenly shattered and as they did every emotion he'd ever buried crashed through him and everything he'd ever thought he believed came tumbling down around him.

Oh, God. No wonder he was in such a state. No wonder he couldn't sleep at night and couldn't think straight. He wanted a lot more than a fling with Laura. He wanted everything. Because he was in love with her. Deeply and completely.

The knowledge slammed into his head and he began to shake. Hell. When had *that* happened? When had the idea of going back to his previous life become so unappealing?

And how did Laura feel about him? Could he dare hope that she loved him back? His mind shot back to the look in her eyes, the one that had put the fear of God into him, just before she'd left. God, she did. Matt's heart began to soar and then plummeted.

Or at least she had.

His stomach churned with dread. Laura was the best thing that had ever happened to him and he'd let her leave. How could he have done that? Because he was terrified of screwing up again? Of pouring everything he had into a relationship and watching it crumble to dust?

But that wouldn't happen with Laura, would it? What

he'd had with Alicia would never have lasted. They'd been too young and had wanted entirely different things out of life. Ultimately he'd called off the engagement because he'd discovered he actually preferred working to spending time with her. Ultimately he hadn't loved her enough.

But with Laura, he loved her so much. And he'd behaved appallingly.

Realisations pummelled through him, each one thudding into his brain hot on the heels of another, making him feel quite weak. What was the point of wanting to return to his previous life when it suddenly seemed empty and lonely? What was the point of clinging on to his business when he wanted to stay on Sassania? And what was the point of having that big old house in Little Somerford, sitting there empty and neglected?

In fact without her, what was the point of anything?

Matt harnessed all the emotions suddenly pounding through him, set his jaw and ran back in the direction of the palace. He'd acted like a prize idiot and it was high time he started putting things right. He could only hope he hadn't left it too late.

CHAPTER THIRTEEN

'PIZZA, Chinese or Indian?' said Kate, sitting next to Laura on the sofa and holding up a fan of menus.

Laura continued zapping mindlessly through the TV channels. 'I don't mind,' she said listlessly. 'You choose. I'm not that hungry.'

Kate gently took the remote control out of Laura's hand, got up from the sofa and planted herself cross-legged on the floor between her and the television. 'Laura, you have to eat.'

'I do eat.' A bit. When she remembered. But to be honest her appetite for food had vanished. As had her appetite for most things. Like getting up in the morning. Fresh air. Breathing even. In fact there didn't seem much point to anything any more.

'More than a couple of slices of toast a day,' Kate said shrewdly.

Laura sighed. 'I know. And I will. It's just that at the moment I feel so…so…' She couldn't finish the sentence. Couldn't voice all the stuff that was churning around inside her. The pain, the emptiness, the yearning and so much more besides. 'Hollow,' she said eventually, blinking away the tears that stung the backs of her eyes.

'Pizza it is, then,' said Kate, tossing the other menus

down and waving the remaining one at Laura. 'Pizza's filling, and always good at a time of crisis. As is wine.'

Laura gave her a wan smile. 'Thank you,' she said. 'And thank you for letting me stay.'

'No problem.'

'Sorry for being such lousy company.'

'Don't worry about it. It's completely understandable. Now what would you like?'

Laura hiccoughed as surprise momentarily lightened her heart. Kate was actually asking her instead of steamrollering ahead. Wow. Maybe more things had changed than just her. It was a shame Matt hadn't and wouldn't.

'The usual,' she said, too dazed and mixed up to bother with something new.

'OK,' said Kate, picking up the phone and hitting the speed dial. 'Hello? Yes. I'd like to place an order…'

Laura listened to Kate rattling off their selection and felt a deep gratitude to her friend. Ever since her plane had touched down a week ago, and what a miserable journey that had been, she'd been operating on automatic.

Unable to bear the thought of going back to the village where the manor house would keep reminding her of Matt—not that she needed reminding when he'd taken up pretty much permanent residence in her head—she'd gone straight to London and had turned up on Kate's doorstep, watery-eyed and shaking.

She'd spilled out the whole sorry story, at which point Kate had enveloped her in a huge hug and pulled her inside, and had been plying her with wine and sympathy ever since.

Kate hung up, poured two huge glasses of wine and

handed one to Laura. 'It'll be here in half an hour. Are you going to be all right?'

Laura took a gulp and felt the alcohol hit her stomach. What choice did she have? She had to be all right if she was going to live any kind of life. Matt would never change and she'd be a fool to hope otherwise. 'I expect so. Eventually.'

'Matt's an idiot. But then he's a man, so what can you expect?'

Kate's scathing tone managed to drag a smile to Laura's face but not for long. Because Matt wasn't an idiot, just a gorgeous, sexy, emotionally deluded, infuriatingly obstinate man.

'So what are you going to do?' Kate asked.

Laura stared at the fireplace, as bleak and empty as her heart. 'I'm not sure. Look for a new job, I suppose. And then find somewhere to live.'

'You can stay here as long as you need.'

'Thanks.' She put her wine glass down and gave Kate a shaky smile. It was so tempting to stay in the warm cocoon of Kate's flat for ever, but sooner or later she had to pull herself together.

She'd been back a week and had been wallowing in self-pity all that time. She'd let herself become a mess. The last time she'd looked in the mirror she'd been horrified by what she'd seen. Her hair was lifeless. Her skin was grey and her eyes were flat. But not horrified enough to do anything about it.

But now she was. Enough was enough. She was fed up with constantly feeling so negative. It was high time she started to focus on the positives.

'You know, maybe it's a good thing me and Matt didn't last,' she said.

Kate looked at her doubtfully. 'In what way?'

'Well, I was just beginning to work out who I was and what I wanted. I was actually getting somewhere. So really, the last thing I needed was to get involved with someone. Especially a member of royalty.' She tried a laugh but it came out as a strangled gasp and she cleared her throat. 'I mean, if going out with a normal man makes me feel suffocated, can you imagine what going out with a king would be like?'

'Hmm, I see your point.'

'In fact,' she said firmly, as the alcohol began to take effect on her poor emotionally battered self, 'I'm going to become more like you.'

'Me?' Kate's eyebrows shot up. 'Crikey, really? I wouldn't go that far. I'm a workaholic who's never managed to hold down a relationship.'

'Exactly. You don't take crap from anyone. You're single. And you're happy, aren't you?'

'Well, yes, but—'

'But nothing. I've made my decision. No more men. Ever. And this time I mean it.' She drained her glass. 'You know, I feel better already,' she said.

'I'm not surprised,' Kate replied, glancing at Laura's empty glass and raising her eyebrow.

Yes, that was the solution, thought Laura, jumping to her feet to fish her phone from the depths of her handbag where it was beeping. She couldn't go on like this, moping all over the place. She needed to take charge. A life of celibacy. Emotional austerity. That was what she'd try. It worked for nuns, didn't it?

She'd head home tomorrow and get on with it. She couldn't hole up at Kate's for ever. And if she tried hard, after a while she might be able to wake up in the morning without thinking about Matt. Maybe after a while she might be able to go to bed without thinking about

Matt. And maybe, just maybe, she might get to spend a whole five minutes without thinking about Matt.

And then her heart might start to repair itself.

'You'll see,' she said firmly, flipping open her phone and clicking on her email to read the one that had just popped into her inbox, 'I'll be—oh.'

'What?'

As she scrolled through the message Laura's heart began to lurch all over the place. 'There's an email from Matt.'

Kate leapt up and rushed to her side. 'What does it say?'

'He's given me the house.'

'He's done *what*?'

'He's given me the house,' she echoed. 'I think,' she added, unable to believe what she'd just read.

'What do you mean you think?'

'I'm not sure. I can't think straight. You read it.'

Laura handed her mobile to Kate and crumpled onto the sofa, her mind struggling to make sense of it all. Why would Matt have given her Somerford Manor? Was it some kind of sign? Was he telling her that he'd never change and that she ought to find what she wanted with someone else?

But how was it that they were over yet he could *still* turn her brain into knots?

'Property law isn't my field of expertise,' said Kate finally, 'but this seems pretty comprehensive. He's definitely given you the house.'

Laura swallowed back the lump in her throat. 'Is it legal?'

'It looks like it. He's also given you a six-figure lump sum to do it up.'

'Oh.'

'Whatever his failings, you can't say he's not generous.'

'Only with things that don't matter,' said Laura as her heart began to ache all over again.

'Why would he give you his house?'

'I don't know.'

'Maybe he's winding up his assets here.'

'I doubt it.' His declaration that he had no intention of staying on Sassania still rang in her ears. 'It's probably a tax move or something.'

'Or maybe he knows how much you love it and just wanted you to have it.'

Laura ached. God, how she'd love to believe that. Because hadn't she secretly been hoping that Matt might have realised that he'd made a whopping mistake in dismissing what they'd had so casually? But he'd never think he'd made a mistake so she could stop that tiny flicker of hope. 'That's even less likely.'

'Well, it certainly solves your problem of where to live.'

And be constantly battered by memories of him and everything she'd lost? No chance. 'I couldn't live there.'

'So what are you going to do? Sell it?'

For some reason that didn't appeal either. 'Tell him I don't want it, I suppose.'

'Don't you want it?'

'Not if it doesn't come with him. And it doesn't, does it?'

Kate shook her head. 'The transfer deed is in your name only so it doesn't look like it. I'm sorry.'

Laura shrugged as if disappointment weren't crashing through her. 'Doesn't matter.' She took out her phone and sent a quick reply and then deleted the email. 'There,' she said, her voice shaking a little. 'Done. Crisis over.'

In the meantime, she thought dolefully as the peal of the doorbell rang through the flat, there was always pizza.

CHAPTER FOURTEEN

LAURA had been back home for half an hour yet her cottage felt as unfamiliar as when she'd first moved in. Had it really only been a handful of weeks? she wondered, flicking on the kettle. So much had happened, so much had changed. *She'd* changed.

But one thing hadn't changed. She arrived here bruised and battered from a doomed relationship, and here she was again.

She could tell herself all she liked that she was ready to move on, but the truth was that she wasn't. How could she be when every corner of her heart wrenched and every cell in her body ached?

When would it ever stop? When *would* she be ready to move on?

The doorbell rang and Laura jumped. If that was one of her neighbours asking for a lift, she thought, heading to the front door, they could forget it.

But as she pulled the door back and stared at the figure standing on her doorstep, Laura froze. All her blood drained to her feet and her head went fuzzy. There was a roaring sound in her ears and her breathing shallowed and quickened. She wondered if she might be about to pass out. Thought it might not be such a bad idea.

Because although it was one of her neighbours, she was pretty sure he wasn't there to ask her for a lift.

Matt looked as if he hadn't slept in weeks. His face was haggard and the lines on his face seemed more sharply etched. Her heart tightened with hope and longing and she had to force it not to, because she wasn't going down that road ever again. Blinking away the nausea, she pulled her shoulders back and curled her hands into fists to stop herself from reaching out, running over to him, wrapping her arms around his neck and kissing the life out of him.

Because however much she might wish otherwise, she'd missed him. God, how she'd missed him.

'What are you doing here, Matt?'

'Looking for you.'

'How did you know I was here?'

'I've been waiting for you.'

'Not too long I hope.'

'A while.'

'I've been in London.'

'Ah.'

He leaned against the door frame, his expression inscrutable, and Laura felt herself start to flap. 'What do you want?'

'I'd like to come in.'

Laura's heart began to hammer. Letting him inside her house would be such a bad idea, but if she left him on the doorstep then he'd know how much he still affected her and once again she'd be the one on the back foot.

'Of course. Please,' she said, mustering up the semblance of a smile. 'Do come in. Coffee?'

He stepped over the threshold and Laura felt as if all the oxygen had been sucked out of the hall. 'No. Thank you.'

He walked into her sitting room and stood with his back to the fireplace looking big and dark and gorgeous.

'So,' she said, desperate to fill the crackling silence. 'How's work?'

'Horrendous.'

Good. Hah. There was some justice in the world, after all. 'I'm sorry to hear that,' she said, feeling anything but.

'You should be,' Matt said with the glimmer of a smile that flipped her stomach. 'It's your fault.'

What? 'How is it *my* fault?'

'I haven't been able to get you out of my mind. I haven't been able to concentrate. I haven't been able to do anything much.'

Laura's breath hitched and her heart thumped as that flicker of hope she'd tried so hard to extinguish flared into life. 'That's not my problem.'

'Isn't it?' He sighed and rubbed his face. 'You don't want my house.'

She bit her lip. 'I don't understand why you gave it to me.'

'Don't you?'

'No. I've been going over and over it in my head and I just can't work it out.'

'Can't you? I'd have thought it was simple.'

Simple? Nothing was simple when it came to her and Matt. 'Then think again.'

Matt shrugged. 'I gave it to you because you love it.'

Laura went very still. Felt a rush of pain shooting

through her and bit back a gasp. Oh, she was such a fool. Hadn't she secretly been hoping that he'd given it to her as a sign that he'd changed his mind? 'Well, I don't want it.'

Matt flinched then tilted his head. 'And what about me? Do you want me?'

Laura's heart skipped a beat. What kind of a question was that? She wanted him with every breath she took, with every cell of her body. And he knew that. So what was he trying to do? Torment her even further?

'Absolutely not,' she said, steeling herself against the way his face paled beneath his tan and made her heart clench. 'So I hope you haven't come to try and persuade me back to Sassania. Because nothing on the planet would tempt me to do that. You were right about us,' she said, her need to protect herself from him lending strength to her words and fire to her voice. 'You know it's a good thing you finished our fling when you did, because I've decided that I really don't need another relationship.'

Matt went very still and his whole body tensed. 'Is that really what you think?'

Laura nodded so violently her head nearly came off. 'Absolutely.' Not.

He frowned. Took a step back, hit the fireplace and stumbled. He looked shaken. Uncertain all of a sudden. 'Then it seems I've had a wasted journey. Forget about the house. It was stupid of me. I'm sorry to have interrupted your morning.'

Laura watched him frown, then nod to himself and shove his hands in his pockets. Her heart lurched as realisation dawned and then began to thunder. 'Oh, my God, you were going to persuade me back to Sassania, weren't you?'

Matt's gaze collided with hers, but his eyes were completely unreadable. 'Don't worry about it. I dare say I'll get over it.'

'No, wait.'

He stilled. 'What?'

Ignoring her churning stomach and all the hope and doubt and nerves tangling up inside her, Laura took a deep breath. 'Why did you come here, Matt?'

'To offer you all those things you've just said you don't want.'

At the bleakness in his voice her throat hurt. Her head began to spin. 'But I thought you didn't do relationships.'

'So did I,' he said with a short humourless laugh. 'But then there are a lot of things I thought I didn't do which I apparently now do do.'

'Like what?'

'I sold my business.'

Laura blinked. 'Oh.'

'And my flat.'

'Why?'

'I'm going to stay on Sassania.'

'That's good.'

'I think so.' He sighed and shoved his hands through his hair. 'You were right about that. It's not just a job. It is my duty and my legacy, but apart from that I like it there. The people are good and I want to make things better.'

'You will.'

'Maybe. Who knows?' He shrugged. 'Anyway I should probably be getting back.'

He was leaving? Now? Just when things were getting interesting? No way. 'When you said you were going to offer me all the things I'd just told you I didn't want, what exactly did you mean?'

Matt froze. 'Forget it,' he said flatly.

She bit her lip. 'No.' She'd get to the bottom of what he was trying to say if it was the last thing she did. And knowing his reluctance to talk, it could well be the last thing she did. 'I don't want to forget it. I want you to tell me what you meant.'

'Fine,' he said, his whole body shaking with something that had her heart pounding crazily. 'I love you. I want to marry you. I want to take you back to Sassania and make lots of little Sassanian babies with you. I want you to restore your house so we can spend our summers there. I won't stifle you. Or suffocate you. You can do what you want. Be what you want. You'd never fade into the background. It would be impossible.' He paused, shoved his hands through his hair. 'My life is empty and soulless without you, Laura. I'm sorry I let you leave like that. I'm sorry I was such an idiot. And I'm sorry it's taken me so long to figure it out. But I love you. More than I ever thought possible.'

Laura reeled as the words tumbled out. 'Oh.'

There was a pause. Matt frowned. 'Oh?' he echoed. 'Is that all you have to say?'

'No, no,' she said faintly. 'It's just quite a lot to take in. I wasn't expecting you to be quite so, um, communicative.'

'I've been practising. You should have heard me the first time. You know how much I like talking about feelings.'

'I do.'

'Well, now I'm done.' He frowned and a vulnerability flashed across his face that made her heart ache. 'So what do you think?'

What did she think? She thought that if the happiness bubbling around inside her grew any bigger she'd burst. 'I think that practice makes completely perfect.'

Matt let out a breath. 'Then in that case do you think you can put me out of my misery and tell me how you feel about me?'

Laura smiled. 'I love you. But you already knew that, didn't you?'

He crossed the room, gathered her in his arms and crushed her against him. 'I had hoped. God, I'd hoped. But then when I got that email saying you didn't want the house…' His mouth twisted.

She laid her hand against his cheek and traced his mouth with her thumb until the twist became a smile. 'I didn't know what it meant. I thought it might be a tax break.'

Matt's eyebrows shot up. 'A tax break? I'm not that complicated.'

Not that complicated? Who was he kidding? 'Or a sign that I should find what I've been looking for with someone else, or something.'

'Don't even think about it. If you marry me, I'll make it my life's mission to give you everything you want.'

'Oh, well, when you put it like that, how could I refuse?'

His mouth came down on hers and Laura sank into his kiss. Her arms wound round his neck and their mouths fused together so fiercely, so completely, their hearts hammering so closely that she didn't know where she stopped and he started. By the time Matt lifted his head desire was thumping around her and her whole body felt weak.

'So a relationship, huh?' said Laura, leaning back and looking up at him once she'd got her breath back.

'I know,' Matt murmured, his eyes dark and warm and filled with love. 'And not just a relationship. Marriage. Who'd have thought?'

'Not scared any more?'

'Terrified, actually.'

Laura smiled. 'Me, too. Neither of us is exactly an expert at the things.'

'I guess we'll just have to muddle through together.'

Laura smiled and tugged at his T-shirt. 'Sounds good to me.'

EPILOGUE

One year later…

'So IT's finally finished,' said Matt, wrapping his arms around Laura's waist and drawing her back against him.

Laura let her head drop back and rest on his shoulder as she snuggled into his arms. She felt the last rays of the evening sun warm on her face, and thought she'd never been so happy.

All in all, over the course of the past year, she and Matt had muddled through remarkably well. Matt had got over his reluctance of talking about feelings with surprising enthusiasm and Laura had begun to understand him. Most of the time.

Their wedding six months ago had done wonders for the morale of the country, which was well on the way to recovery. Of course, she hadn't been able to continue working on the palace, but any disappointment she might have felt had been more than compensated by having the manor house to devote her energies to. 'It is,' she said, gazing up at the house she adored. 'What do you think?'

'I think you're amazing,' he said, breath caressing her ear and making her shiver.

Laura grinned. 'Of the house.'

'It's beautiful. You've done a fantastic job.'

'Thank you.'

'You know,' he said, sliding his hands up her body to cup her breasts, 'all that remains now is to work on the hordes of children you think should fill it.'

Laura put her hands over his and lowered them back to her abdomen, then twisted slightly in his arms to smile up at him. 'Funny you should mention that…'

* * * * *

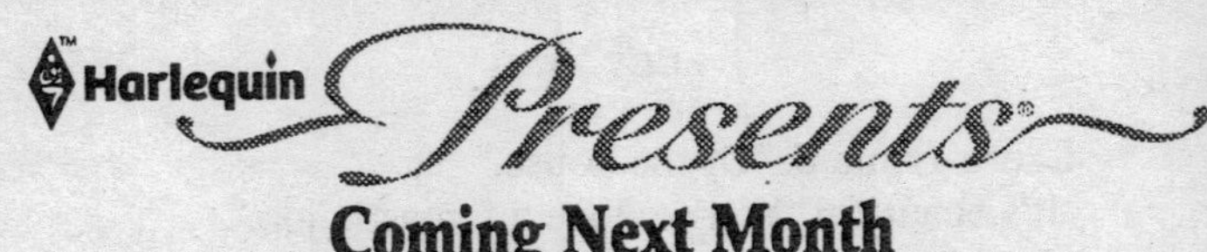

Coming Next Month

from **Harlequin Presents®.** Available September 27, 2011.

#3017 THE COSTARELLA CONQUEST
Emma Darcy

#3018 THE FEARLESS MAVERICK
Robyn Grady
The Notorious Wolfes

#3019 THE KANELLIS SCANDAL
Michelle Reid

#3020 HEART OF THE DESERT
Carol Marinelli

#3021 DOUKAKIS'S APPRENTICE
Sarah Morgan
21st Century Bosses

#3022 AN INCONVENIENT OBSESSION
Natasha Tate

Coming Next Month

from **Harlequin Presents® EXTRA.** Available October 11, 2011.

#169 IN WANT OF A WIFE?
Cathy Williams
The Powerful and the Pure

#170 THE RETURN OF THE STRANGER
Kate Walker
The Powerful and the Pure

#171 THE S BEFORE EX
Mira Lyn Kelly
Tabloid Scandals

#172 SEX, GOSSIP AND ROCK & ROLL
Nicola Marsh
Tabloid Scandals

HPECNM0911

Visit www.HarlequinInsideRomance.com for more information on upcoming titles!

Harlequin Romantic Suspense presents the latest book in the scorching new KELLEY LEGACY *miniseries from best-loved veteran series author Carla Cassidy*

Scandal is the name of the game as the Kelley family fights to preserve their legacy, their hearts...and their lives.

Read on for an excerpt from the fourth title RANCHER UNDER COVER

Available October 2011 from Harlequin Romantic Suspense

"Would you like a drink?" Caitlin asked as she walked to the minibar in the corner of the room. She felt as if she needed to chug a beer or two for courage.

"No, thanks. I'm not much of a drinking man," he replied.

She raised an eyebrow and looked at him curiously as she poured herself a glass of wine. "A ranch hand who doesn't enjoy a drink? I think maybe that's a first."

He smiled easily. "There was a six-month period in my life when I drank too much. I pulled myself out of the bottom of a bottle a little over seven years ago and I've never looked back."

"That's admirable, to know you have a problem and then fix it."

Those broad shoulders of his moved up and down in an easy shrug. "I don't know how admirable it was, all I knew at the time was that I had a choice to make between living and dying and I decided living was definitely more appealing."

She wanted to ask him what had happened preceding that six-month period that had plunged him into the bottom of the bottle, but she didn't want to know too much about him. Personal information might produce a false sense of intimacy that she didn't need, didn't want in her life.

"Please, sit down," she said, and gestured him to the table. She had never felt so on edge, so awkward in her life.

"After you," he replied.

She was aware of his gaze intensely focused on her as she rounded the table and sat in the chair, and she wanted to tell him to stop looking at her as if she were a delectable dessert he intended to savor later.

Watch Caitlin and Rhett's sensual saga unfold amidst the shocking, ripped-from-the-headlines drama of the Kelley Legacy miniseries in

RANCHER UNDER COVER

Available October 2011 only from Harlequin Romantic Suspense, wherever books are sold.

HRSEXP1011